ROYAL HEARTS

ROYAL HEARTS

J.R. SHEPHERD

Contents

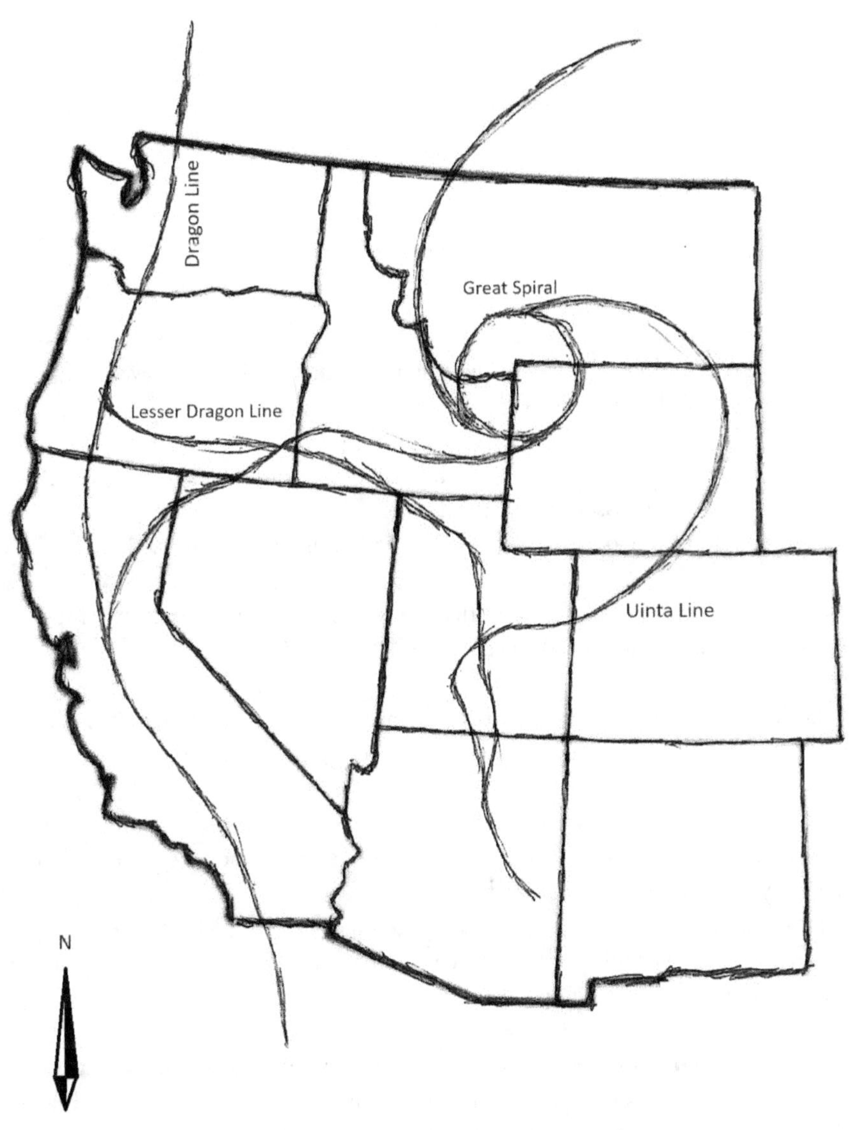

Dragon Line
Great Spiral
Lesser Dragon Line
Uinta Line
N

Glossary

Aether: A very thin substance in ancient and medieval science believed to fill the space not occupied by the terrestrial world.

Aspect: A person who has inherited the blood or power of an animal, often gaining abilities or senses associated with that animal. Most abilities are minor, except for those with the blood of animals associated with the signs of the Zodiac.

Channels: Paths within the body that carry energy in a way similar to the way blood is carried through blood vessels.

Leyline: A flowing 'river' that carries the natural energy produced by the Earth. Functions the same way that Channels do, but on a global scale.

Outer Magic: Magic that is not part of the natural order of the world. Mostly consists of any power used by, or given through, spirits or other entities that do not normally inhabit the physical world.

Veve: A religious symbol used in Vodou as a beacon to call a specific spirit or as a representation of that spirit during rituals.

Vodou: Sometimes called Voodoo, Vodou is a religion based on several western and central African religions and Roman Catholicism. Can be practiced safely under most circumstances, but can become a source of Outer Magic.

Wicca: Also known as simply 'The Craft', Wicca is a religious system of magic that works with natural energy and the basics of how the world works. One of only a small number of magic systems outside of Sorcery that is not a type of Outer Magic.

Prologue

The children marched along the silent halls, held in a magical trance by the teachers that guided them. The dozens of little feet shuffled quietly on the cold stone floors as they climbed the north tower steps to the Pylon. A heavy stone door was pushed open and the children filed into a small round amphitheater and stood at even intervals all around the room.

Floating above a short stone column at the center was the Pylon. A large clear crystal, the shape of a diamond, turning slowly on its axis, and glowing with its own otherworldly light.

"Is everything ready?" A man entered the room and the stone door slipped quietly shut behind him. He seemed young, with jet black hair and sharp blue eyes. He was thin and not what anyone would describe as tall.

"It is, Headmaster." Answered one of the female teachers in hushed tones. "But you do not have to oversee the ceremony yourself sir. Julia is used to acting as the Focus and your schedule is very busy." The Headmaster smiled and shook his head.

"I am not so busy I cannot see to my own students. Besides, this drawing feels different, special somehow. How many foundlings do we have this time?" The Headmaster's eyes gazed expertly over the faces of all the small children, most no more than eight. The teacher turned to watch as well.

"Seven from Utah, nine from out of state, the rest were unknown. Twenty three altogether, fewer than usual. This class will be very small." The Headmaster nodded.

"Which is as it should be. No child should be abandoned or feared for abilities as precious as these."

The teacher nodded her agreement. The room lightened almost imperceptibly from the frosted glass ceiling.

"The moon has risen Headmaster. Will that cause a problem?" The Headmaster shook his head and waved one hand with a muttered word. Thick, velvety darkness slid across the moon behind the glass and the room darkened until only the light from the Pylon kept the darkness at bay.

"No problem at all. Prepare for the first draw." The handful of teachers among the children directed them to sit on the steps of the amphitheater and then lined the walls of the room and raised their arms to either side, touching the fingertips of the person on either side of them.

The Headmaster, with his back to the door, raised both his hands in the air as if to cradle the children below him. When he spoke, his voice rumbled across the room like the thunder from a far away storm.

"First draw, The Base of Power. Show us the elements that guide these small one's hands."

The clear crystal became cloudy and it's light became fractured. The cards sitting at it's base spread out into the room as if carried by a slow whirlwind, it's twisting path through the air chaotic, with no discernible pattern.

"Draw."

As the Headmaster's voice flowed over the room, each child raised their hand and plucked a card from the air before them. The unchosen cards continued to spin through the air. The Headmaster brought his hands together in front of him and spoke again.

"Second draw, The Form of Power. Show us the forms that these small ones will mold."

The crystal flashed, as if a small storm were brewing within, and the cards began to race faster through the air.

"Draw."

The children reached into the air and easily grasped a second card. A second flash changed the crystal blue.

"These children will be powerful spellcasters." The female teacher whispered from her place next to the Headmaster. He nodded and then slid his hands down his arms and across his body to his shoulders, a faint golden glow settling around him.

"Third draw, Final draw, The Path of Power. Show us the Fate of these small one's hearts."

The clouds within The Pylon boiled and lightning lanced through them. The cards flew through the air with a steady hum. One by one each child reached into the air, poised to take their card. The Headmaster waited for several moments, eyes closed, waiting for some unknown sign.

"Draw."

The children immediately snatched a card from the rapidly spinning mass, and a rumble shook the room. The Pylon itself cleared almost instantly and turned a brilliant, fiery red, showering the room with incorporeal pink sparks.

"What is happening Headmaster?" The female teacher beside him asked, concern coloring her voice. The Headmaster folded his arms and leaned his back against the cold stone door. After a few moments he answered.

"The King and Queen of Hearts were chosen."

A collective gasp rippled across the room, but the spell keeping the children in a trance did not waver.

"A King and Queen? But of the same suit? At the same time? And the same Pylon? That's unheard of! Can two people, who are so young, already truly be drawn together by fate?"

The Headmaster nodded and motioned with his hand. The darkness that had shrouded the room lifted and the moon's soft light filtered down on them, fading the Pylon back to flawless clarity and turning the sparks in the air into light wisps that quickly disappeared.

"Find the cards, and we will see who drew them."

He opened his eyes as the teachers left their vigilant posts along the walls and carefully checked each child. Eventually two teachers each stopped next to a child and raised their hands. The Headmaster nodded.

"Take the other children and their cards to their rooms. I will handle these two myself."

The teachers all bowed and then ushered the rest of the children out of the room, leaving only a young boy and a young girl sitting in the room alone with the Headmaster.

He waited quietly until the sound of the other children and teachers faded away, then he moved the two children together and touched their foreheads. Both blinked several times and looked around groggily, as if waking from a deep sleep.

"You are safe, little ones." The Headmaster told them kindly. "I do not know the circumstances that brought you here, and it does not matter. From this day forward this place will be your home. Everyone here is your family now, and you will be taken care of."

The young man looked at the three cards in his hands and ran his thumb over the King of Hearts that lay on top of the other two. The little girl looked numb and didn't seem to realize she also held three cards.

"You will come to understand the significance of your cards in time. For now, you may call me your Master. I will do my best to teach and care for you both. It is time to sleep, tomorrow brings new light and with it, a new life."

* * *

A middle aged woman, with blonde hair and green eyes, watched as the new students filed into the room and sat down on rows of chairs.

"Good morning everyone. I am Deputy Headmaster Julia. I know some of you may be a bit confused, as you were brought here over the past few days with little warning. I first wish to express that you are all safe and welcome here, so do not hesitate to ask any of your teachers if you have questions."

Julia paused for a moment to ensure that the students had understood. After receiving a few silent nods, she continued.

"Secondly, I would like to address your cards. Many of you had your ceremony last night, but a few of you have had private ceremonies. It is the rule at this school that you do not discuss your cards. There are many reasons for this rule, but you are all very young and it may be difficult to understand so please take care to follow it anyway. Please ask a teacher if you wish to know more."

She paused again until she received nods from everyone.

"I'm glad to see you all understand. That said, I am certain you must all be curious about what your cards mean. I will do my best to quickly go over them, but again, please ask your teachers if you have any further questions.

Firstly, your cards, and the order you drew them in, will help us determine how best to teach each of you as individuals. There are many disciplines of Sorcery and each suit is unique in how it interacts with your power. The numbers tell us how proficient you could become with that magic. Most of you will have drawn cards that are fours or fives, but there is no cause for concern if your numbers are higher or lower.

As for the suits:

Spades are warriors, defenders. They are good with casting magic without speaking words aloud, and excel in combat.

Hearts represent a journey of growth. They are good at manipulating the elements, but are uniquely suited to working alongside others.

Clubs are able to easily understand others. They can commune well with nature, and make excellent healers.

Diamonds are scholars. They excel at low level magic, but struggle with high level magic. But this loss of strength is made up for in their insight and ability to perceive the world around them.

This is a very basic explanation of the four suits. Again, we must not discuss our cards here, but if you have any questions your teachers will be happy to help you."

Julia could tell that only a handful of students seemed interested in her explanation. She smiled, trying to remember what it was like to be so young.

"That is all you need to hear from me. A teacher will now take you around the school and show you where the classrooms and other necessities are. And from myself and the Headmaster, welcome to The Academy."

I

Chapter One

Leo sat quietly in the school library, skimming through the large leather bound tome in front of him, trying to find information for his report on multi-person spellcasting. He could hear a few people in one corner talking about something he couldn't quite make out. He tried ignoring them as best he could as he flipped through the pages, but eventually gave up and closed the tome.

"Wonder if Temmy might know." Leo muttered to himself, scratching the back of his head and straightening his short brown hair before standing up with a groan.

He lifted the heavy tome and rested it on his shoulder, making his way over to the shelves where he had gotten it and heaving it back into place. He looked at the tome for a few moments and then sighed, turning away and hoping he wouldn't have to come back and pull it back off the shelf again.

He left the library, hearing the two girls near the door mention something about hiding out during the next full moon as he went, and turned to head towards the cafeteria.

It was relatively quiet in the halls, as everyone but the seniors were still in classes, so Leo managed to make it to the cafeteria without running into anyone. He walked in and went straight to the lunch lady, who held out a tray.

"And how are you today young man?" The gray haired woman asked. "Getting some studying done during your free period?" Leo shook his head and smiled back, taking the tray.

"No, I was trying to find some information in the library, but I wasn't having any luck." Leo reached down and grabbed a pre-cut submarine roll, putting it on his tray and opening it up. The lunch lady nodded with a crooked grin.

"Well, get some food in you and try again. I'm sure you'll find what you need once you have a full belly." Leo nodded as he stacked some sliced cheese and deli meat on his roll.

"Thanks, I'm sure I'll find it eventually." He slid his tray further down the line, acting like he was adding lettuce to his sandwich so the lunch lady wouldn't yell at him about eating his vegetables.

He grabbed several cookies and a carton of milk at the end of the line and then turned towards the opposite end of the cafeteria. The large room was mostly empty, with only a handful of people scattered among the various tables.

Leo scanned the tables and quickly spotted two girls sitting at a far corner table. He made his way over, watching as one of the girls with long, golden brown hair motioned with a pencil to something in a notebook. The second girl, with shorter red hair and round glasses nodded, quietly listening to whatever was being said.

"I was hoping I would find the two of you here." Leo called out as he approached. He slid his tray onto the table opposite the two girls and plopped himself onto the attached bench.

"What makes you think we wanted to be found?" The long haired girl asked sarcastically. Leo pouted, reaching for his milk.

"That's so mean Izzy. And here I was, genuinely glad to see you." The long haired girl stuck her nose in the air with a loud harrumph, but struggled to hide the smile growing on her face.

"We weren't exactly hiding." The short haired girl said quietly.

"Temmy, you are a gentleman and a scholar. Good afternoon by the way. Would you like a cookie?" Leo held out a cookie, but it got snatched by the long haired girl who promptly took a large bite out of it.

"I thought you said you thought the cookies in the cafeteria were bland, Isabella." Temmy watched the long haired girl chew and subconsciously took the second cookie Leo offered her.

Leo chuckled.

"Izzy likes to complain about the food, but she won't turn down snacks if they're available." Isabella scowled at him as she tried to hurry and swallow her cookie so she could complain at him. Leo pulled his tray closer to himself and wrapped an arm around it, as if to protect his sandwich and remaining cookie, and scowled back.

Isabella reached out and snatched his milk carton, and used it to wash down her cookie before he could stop her.

"Hey! How am I supposed to wash down my sandwich now?" Leo whined.

Isabella wiped her mouth off and handed him the carton back.

"I didn't drink all of it, you'll be fine." Leo frowned at the milk carton, holding it at arms length and tipping it slightly to try and look inside. He gave Isabella a side eyed look and slowly pulled the milk closer to his face, giving the opening of the carton a loud sniff.

Isabella laughed at him.

"You big baby, it's fine. I didn't spit in it or anything." Leo sighed in defeat and picked up his sandwich, taking a large bite out of one end. Isabella turned back to Temmy.

"Well, back to what I was saying before we were so rudely interrupted. Do you think I need to change the tone of the paper? It's supposed to be an argument on the ethics of public displays of magic, but I don't really want it to sound combative." Temmy shook her head and pushed the notebook in front of her back over to Isabella.

"No, I think it sounds fine. If anything, it almost sounds a bit defensive. It might make the argument come across better if you made your statements more direct, but the overall tone doesn't really need to change."

Leo grunted suddenly, trying to say something around his sandwich, but failing. He grabbed his milk, pausing just long enough to scowl sideways at Isabella again, and quickly washed down his food.

"I almost forgot why I came over here." He said, setting his milk back on the table and wiping his mouth.

"Wasn't it because you wanted to see our beautiful faces?" Isabella asked.

Leo took a deep breath, then paused for a second.

"I plead the fifth." He said, then quickly turned to talk to Temmy before Isabella could respond with anything more than a sputter.

"I was trying to find information on multi-person casting in the library earlier, but I couldn't find what I was looking for. Do you happen to know, off hand, if there is any specific limit to the number of people who can participate in a given spell?" Temmy tilted her head slightly, staring blankly at the table, ordering her internal library of thoughts.

"I don't believe so. The burden on the person who acts as the Dom or Focus will grow based on how many people are assisting in casting the spell. Though how many people each individual is capable of working with is different for everyone. Not to mention that multiple people can act as a Focus in a single spell to reduce the strain on any individual. Theoretically, you can just have as many people acting as Focus as you need to assist in casting, so there should be no limit on how many people can actually participate in total. Of course, working with someone you are familiar with will always be better than working with several people you don't know." Leo nodded.

"That's kind of what I thought, but I wasn't a hundred percent sure. It doesn't help that Headmaster Orpheus is traveling right now, so I couldn't go ask him, and the library wasn't much help either. Thanks for the help Temmy."

"Sure. Glad I could help." Temmy answered quietly while carefully avoiding eye contact with everyone.

Leo reached for his sandwich and opened his mouth to say something else, but was interrupted by a thump and a soft skittering sound. He looked down on the bench next to him and watched a slightly rotund, slick black salamander trying to leap up from the floor. It half landed on the bench next to him with another thump, then flailed its hind legs around, trying to drag itself the rest of the way up.

Leo reached down and lifted the salamander up and put him on the table. The salamander lay flat on the table for several moments, breathing rapidly.

"You poor thing, where did you come from?" Isabella asked, scratching the salamander's chin with one finger.

The salamander looked at her for a moment, then turned its head to look at Temmy. After a few seconds it turned itself around and looked at Leo.

Several seconds of staring seemed to allow the salamander to identify Leo as the one it was looking for, and it skittered a few steps over the table and then rolled over onto its back, revealing a folded piece of parchment paper stuck to it's belly.

Leo reached out and peeled the paper away from the salamander, who then flipped itself back over. It took a moment to look around again, then skittered along the table and rested itself against Temmy's arm.

"Oh, um, hello." Temmy said, uncertainly. The Salamander twisted its head a bit to look at her, then closed its eyes and laid flat on the table against her arm.

"Look how tired he is. Someone must have sent him a long way to deliver that message." Isabella leaned over to try and pet the salamander again, but then noticed Leo was frowning slightly.

"Hey, what's up?" She asked him, waiting several seconds for him to read the full message.

"Headmaster Orpheus wants me to go look into something. Said he won't be back for a little while and wants me to see to it for him."

Leo sighed, muttering a word under his breath and waving the parchment in the air. The paper burst into flames and disappeared in an instant.

"Is everything ok? Do you need help with anything?" Isabella asked. Leo shook his head and stood.

"No, everything's fine. Just means I'll be pulling a late night tonight so I can get my report written. But that shouldn't be too bad since Temmy gave me the info I needed. Thanks again by the way."

Temmy shook her head.

"No need to thank me." Leo placed his hands in the small of his back and leaned back, stretching with a groan.

"Welp," He said, grabbing his sandwich and quickly chugging the rest of his milk. "Me and my sandwich are leaving. Farewell. Temmy, keep Izzy out of trouble for me."

"Maybe worry about keeping yourself out of trouble." Isabella shot back with a growl, and Leo made a point to leap away from the table with a gasp.

"So scary. Run away!" He cried before sprinting cartoonishly through the cafeteria door.

Isabella grumbled, pulling Leo's tray over to her.

"I wish he wouldn't try to hide things from me." She complained before taking the last cookie off the tray and taking a bite out of it. Temmy watched the salamander, still napping against her arm.

"I think he just doesn't want you to worry. I'm sure the Headmaster wouldn't ask him to do anything terrible." Isabella sighed.

"I know, but it's serious enough for him to leave immediately. He is also skipping his afternoon classes, which he never does, and he didn't even take the time to finish eating. He eats really fast too, so that makes me feel like it's even more serious than he makes it out to be. He is too childish for someone who just turned eighteen and it ticks me off, so much."

Isabella aggressively shoved the remaining bit of cookie in her mouth, scowling as she chewed. Temmy waited until she was done chewing and swallowed before speaking.

"Speaking of him bothering you, why do you still let him call you Izzy?" Temmy asked tentatively, trying to act as if she was more focused on the salamander. "You have always hated people shortening your name."

Isabella grumbled some more.

"I don't know. Maybe it's because everything he says is annoying, so the name thing doesn't stand out so much with him."

Temmy took another breath to speak, then decided against it. Instead she slowly pulled away from the salamander, who opened it's eyes and turned its head to look up at her.

"I'm sorry." She told it, a little upset. "I have to go to class now."

Isabella almost jumped off of the bench.

"Class! I was so angry at Leo I almost forgot about classes. And now I realize I'm going to have to take extra notes so I can give them to Leo when he gets back."

Isabella grabbed the tray and threw the empty milk carton on it to take back to the lunch lady.

"Oh, he's going to owe me big time. He better appreciate it."

Temmy considered telling her that taking extra notes was probably unnecessary, but shook her head and said nothing. She spared one more apologetic glance for the salamander and then followed Isabella, listening to her rant as they made their way towards their first afternoon class.

* * *

Isabella listened to her Outer Magics teacher drone on and on about the root origins of specific members of The Fae Court. Both of her hands held a pencil and scribbled identical notes in two separate notebooks laid out on her desk. She mindlessly turned the pages once they filled and continued writing without missing a word, all while trying to memorize everything being said.

"The Fae Queen has been referenced in many ancient texts, including texts containing lists of pact holders claiming to have made deals with her to gain some form of power. In these ancient texts, the Fae Queen herself is mentioned by many names, and quite often just by her title as Queen. It wasn't until 1595 that the name Titania became popular after it's use in Shakespeare's 'A Midsummer Night's Dream' made it a common, and well known, reference to the Queen of Fairies."

The teacher spoke in an almost monotone voice, and Isabella could tell most other students in the class were not paying attention. The only other person even taking notes was Temmy a few seats ahead of Isabella, and a handful of other students had been lulled entirely to sleep.

A low bell rang out, resonating throughout the halls of the school.

"That's all for today everyone." The teacher continued to drone. "Remember to finish your reading assignments tonight. There will be a quiz tomorrow on The Fae Court and their most famous interactions with our world. Also, the dangers of dealing with the spirit worlds in general."

Isabella heard several groans around the room as she finished off both sets of her notes. She closed both notebooks and stuffed both of them into her bag. She half bowed to the teacher as they left the room and then stood up from her desk and walked over to Temmy.

"I didn't realize how ambiguous the Fae Court was. They have only ever taught basic stories in class before." Isabella leaned against Temmy's desk as she spoke, looking down at the notes she had meticulously kept.

"The Fae are mostly tricksters who want to appear as mysterious as possible." Temmy said quietly, filling out a small diagram on her notes as she spoke. "It's harder to trick people if they are knowledgeable about the Fae and the rules for interacting with them." Isabella turned around and sat on the edge of the desk.

"I guess so. Though I still feel like that might be something important to learn before senior year." Temmy finished her notes and closed her notebook.

"It's because the Fae are a source of Outer Magic. The Academy wants children who are learning to learn the magic they are attuned to before they learn about the powers that mortals have tried to use outside of personal magic. They don't want a young child to get frustrated with their studies and try to seek out a dangerous alternative that they think might be easier." Temmy slid out of her seat and Isabella pushed herself away from the desk.

"That makes sense. I could see people getting frustrated after failing to cast a spell a few too many times."

"It only makes sense if you're too dumb to figure it out yourself."

A voice said out loud beside them. Temmy frowned and tried to hide herself behind Isabella.

Isabella whirled around and faced a young man sitting on his desk with his feet up on the back of his chair. The young man was tall and slim, with soft black hair that had coppery undertones.

"Titus, you are a fool if you think there isn't a single student in the Academy who hasn't struggled at some point. Yourself included." Isabella scowled at him and he laughed.

"I'm actually gifted with magic, unlike the seemingly endless number of Artless peasants that attend this sad excuse for a school." He leaned back trying to stare down Temmy, clearly directing his condescending tone at her.

Isabella felt her fists clench and was ready to push past the desk in front of her and grab Titus by the collar, but she felt Temmy pulling on the back of her shirt to get her to drop it. Isabella took a deep breath to get a hold of herself.

"You are no better than anyone else here, Titus, no matter what family you come from. Just because you have a bunch of lackeys who try to suck up to you doesn't mean you are worth anything." Titus smirked and spun around, sliding off his desk and standing at his full height.

"Well aren't you feisty today. By the way, where is your little friend? Didn't see him in any classes this afternoon. The poor baby feeling sick to his tummy?" Titus pouted and spoke the last in a baby voice.

Isabella drew herself up as tall as she could, ignoring Temmy's continued tugging.

"Sick of you maybe. Why would I know where Leo is? I'm not his keeper, and I couldn't care less what he's up to." Titus continued to smirk.

"Oh is that so? Wouldn't be surprised if he was hiding. He's scared of getting in a fight with a real sorcerer." Isabella turned and took Temmy by the shoulders and directed her towards the door.

"No, Headmaster Orpheus told both of us explicitly to avoid getting into fights with other students. Especially you, since you always seem like you're trying to start something." As they reached the door and Temmy walked out Isabella paused for a moment and half turned back.

"However, if I ever hear you call any other students Artless again, I might just forget about all the rules I was asked to follow."

Isabella turned and rushed out of the room after Temmy so Titus wouldn't have time to respond with something that might set her off. She caught up with Temmy and followed her until they made it down the hall and around a corner.

"One of these days I'm going to lose it and blow up a classroom with him in it." Isabella did her best not to yell too loudly, but her hands were clenched so tightly they were shaking.

"Try not to think about it too much. He is a bully, and he just wants to try and get under people's skin." Temmy spoke with her head pointed squarely at the floor. Isabella shook her head.

"It wouldn't be nearly so bad if he didn't always pick on you, Temmy. And to call someone, anyone, Artless. He is the lowest sort of scum." Isabella had to pause to take a deep breath to try and calm down.

"Well, I'm not exactly good at magic..." Temmy tried to mutter under her breath. She gasped as Isabella stepped in front of her and grabbed her face, forcing her look up and meet her gaze.

"Don't, for even one second, believe you aren't good at magic. You may not be good at casting high level spells, but there is almost no one in the school with a grasp of cantrips and auras as good as yours. Plus you are an ideal companion for group spellcasting. Not to mention there probably isn't a single person in the school as knowledgeable as you." Isabella glanced over her shoulder to make sure no one was within earshot, then leaned closer and spoke in almost a whisper.

"I know we aren't supposed to share our cards, but anyone who pays attention and cares even a little could see at least one of your cards is a strong Diamond."

Temmy's eyes widened and Isabella let go of her face.

"So don't let people like Titus tell you that you aren't worth anything. If I was ever in trouble I would take you at my side over him any day."

Temmy nodded slowly, her eyes wet with sudden tears being held back. One corner of her mouth turned upward in a slight smile, a rare occurrence that always put a smile on Isabella's face.

"Thank you Isabella. I'm glad you are my friend." Isabella laughed and threw her arms around Temmy and squeezed.

"You are my favorite person Temmy, I always will be your friend." Temmy sniffled once and let Isabella hold onto her for a moment before speaking a few muffled words into her chest.

"Whenever you are done, I would like to breath again." Isabella gasped and jumped back, letting go of Temmy, who straightened her glasses.

Temmy half smiled, and Isabella laughed, and they both continued walking down the hall towards the private dorm rooms.

"You shouldn't sell yourself short though." Temmy said quietly. Isabella blinked a couple times in surprise.

"What do you mean?" She turned her head to look at Temmy as they walked.

"I just think you are also one of the smartest people in the school. And the only person I can think of off the top of my head who can keep up with you practically would be Leo."

Isabella shook her head.

"Oh I wouldn't say that. I'm just good at taking notes. And Leo... well... I'm not sure how he does it. He doesn't really seem to put much time or effort into studying. Maybe he crams when no one else is watching?"

Temmy nodded her agreement.

"Maybe. Though your note taking is kind of... intimidating."

Isabella opened her mouth to complain about that comment, but snapped it shut again as they rounded the last corner to the dorms and caught sight of Leo.

Leo trudged slowly towards the door that led up to the private rooms, dragging his feet as he went. He was pale, and looked exhausted, but managed a dopey looking grin when he saw the two girls.

"Oh heeey, fancy meeting you here." He tried to sound sarcastic, but

Isabella could still hear that he was basically ready to collapse where he stood.

"I could say the same to you, but seeing as we live across the hall from each other I wouldn't exactly call it surprising seeing you here after class." Isabella gave a snarky reply, but quickened her pace just in case she needed to prevent him from falling over. Temmy was right behind her, and quickly opened the door that led up the stairs.

"You look tired, what happened? Was the headmaster's task something really difficult?" Temmy motioned for Leo to go through the door as she spoke. Leo stepped through, but instead of heading up the stairs, he grabbed the door, and stepped aside so the girls could pass.

"Not so much difficult as tedious. Probably had me do it just so he wouldn't have to when he gets back."

Isabella frowned, but let Temmy go up the stairs ahead of them, and closed the door after stepping through so she could force Leo to go up first. They locked eyes for a few moments before Leo sighed tiredly.

"Age before beauty today I guess." Isabella slapped his shoulder, though gently, and turned him to face the stairs.

"Get up there before I conjure something unpleasant to take you up." Leo started up the stairs with a grunt.

"So rude." He said, keeping one hand on the railing.

Isabella followed close behind, one hand on the rail, and one hand poised to catch Leo if he started to fall back.

"You're right, I wouldn't want to scare Temmy when we get to the top."

Leo chuckled.

"That would be awful."

After what felt like hours of walking, they reached the top and made their way down past the first few doors. Temmy walked back out into the hall, having already opened her and Isabella's room and dropped off her bag.

"Do you have your key with you? I can get the door for you." Temmy offered once they reached her.

"Thank you Temmy, you are a saint. But the door isn't locked, so it's fine." Leo sounded a bit winded.

"You left your door unlocked again?" Isabella asked, clearly exasperated. Leo shrugged, turning the handle and swinging the door open.

"I don't really have anything worth stealing." He said, stepping inside.

Isabella made a face and made strangling motions behind him. Temmy suppressed a smile and went back into their room.

Isabella followed Leo into his room and found him already reclined in an old chair, head tilted back with his eyes closed. She watched him sit motionless for several moments before reaching into her bag to take out one of her notebooks.

"You probably should close the door if you are going to sleep like that."

"Oh, didn't I?" Leo grumbled, his eyes still closed.

Isabella frowned and tilted her head to one side.

"Do you have anything to eat? Temmy and I are making a meat pie tonight, do you want me to bring you some?"

Leo slowly shook his head.

"No, I have some stuff. I don't want you two to go out of your way to have to bring me anything. I'll just take a nap for a bit and then grab something." His words were kind of breathy and trailing off like he was half asleep already.

Isabella waited several more moments before speaking again.

"Are you sure you're all right?" Leo halfheartedly waved one hand.

"I'm great, never been better." Isabella walked over and tossed the notebook in Leo's lap before leaning over and bracing herself on the arms of the chair, leaning forward to get to eye level with him.

"I mean it Leo, you look awful. it's like you haven't slept or eaten anything in a week, even though I watched you eat earlier today. Temmy is worried about you too."

Leo took a deep breath and then let it out slowly. He tipped his head forward, opening his eyes and looking directly into Isabella's.

They sat in silence for several moments, just staring, Isabella noticing something intense and almost sharp in the depths of Leo's eyes.

"I will be ok." He finally spoke, all traces of sarcasm gone from his tired voice. "I promise there isn't anything to worry about. Just a lot of magical focusing I had to do for the Headmaster. A good night of sleep and I will be back to normal."

Isabella searched his eyes, hoping to find some trace of a lie, and he quietly met her gaze until she finally sighed and pushed away from the chair.

"Alright. The notebook has notes from the classes you missed today. There is a test tomorrow in Outer Magics, so you should probably go over those notes first." Leo put on another dopey grin.

"Thanks. I'd be lost without you."

Isabella turned with a scoff.

"And don't you forget it. I'll bring over the leftover meat pie after Temmy and I are done, so you better not let any of it go to waste."

She marched out of the room, closing the door behind her.

Leo watched her go out of the corner of his eye so he wouldn't have to turn his head and, once he heard her door across the hall close, he closed his eyes again.

"Thank you." He muttered quietly, almost immediately starting to doze off. "I don't deserve it, but thank you."

2

Chapter Two

Isabella watched Leo exchange a few words with their Outer Magics professor while handing in his test.

After a moment the professor nodded and Leo bowed before heading back to his desk. He grabbed his bag and slung it over his shoulder, giving Isabella a stupid looking grin as he passed her.

"Good luck with the rest of your test." He whispered in a tone that made her immediately want stab him with her pencil as he passed.

Isabella glanced back over her shoulder and watched as Leo's grin was replaced by a determined frown as he quietly slipped through the classroom door. She turned back and immediately started filling out the last pages of her test. She felt, more than saw, several other people stand up and take their tests to the front. Some of them returned quietly to their seats, and some went out to stand in the hall while everyone else finished.

Once she was finished, Isabella gathered up all her things and took her test to the professor.

"I have a few things I need to go get done," She whispered to the professor as she handed him her test. "Could I leave early today?" The Professor quickly flipped through her test to make sure everything was filled out.

"Everything looks fine with your test. That's fine. I'm sure you and Leo have a lot going on with the Headmaster still traveling." Even his whisper somehow managed to sound like a drone.

Isabella bowed.

"Thank you professor, I promise I will come in early Monday to get my test and go over anything I missed."

The professor nodded and Isabella turned and hurried out of the room.

Isabella headed straight towards her room, hoping that Leo would head to his room to put his bag away before leaving to do whatever he was planning on doing. She almost didn't notice the person leaning against the upper room door when she came around the corner, but stopped short once she saw him.

Titus had his arms crossed over his chest, with a self important smirk on his face.

"I was hoping you might come by here after class. Got a proposition for you." Isabella frowned and closed the distance.

"Not interested. Now, out of the way. I need to get to my room and then I have work to do." Titus scoffed, continuing to lean against the door.

"You sure? It's a once in a lifetime opportunity." Isabella shook her head.

"I want nothing to do with anything to do with you. I don't care if it was an opportunity to become ruler of the world or some other equally grand design. Now move. I won't ask nicely again, and I am not in the mood for arguing today." She held her right hand out slightly, making it clear she would use force if he didn't listen.

Titus's smirk lessened, but he pushed himself away from the door.

"Suit yourself."

Isabella opened the door, barely waiting long enough for Titus to move out of the way, and slipped through, rushing up to her room.

Isabella unlocked her door and took a step inside to toss her bag across the room onto a chair. She locked her door again and closed it, immediately moving across the hallway to knock on Leo's door. She waited several seconds and then knocked again. After a minute or two with no reply she tested the door knob.

The door swung open and she stuck her head inside to look around. Everything was quiet and the lights were all off, some dishes from what she assumed was Leo's breakfast still sitting on a small table in the kitchenette.

"You here Leo?" She called, hoping she would get an answer. No answer came. She grumbled and closed the door.

She turned towards the stairs, then thought of Titus, and decided to go up and check the Headmaster's office before going out through the second story entrance.

Isabella quickly moved down to the end of the hall and politely knocked on the oak double doors of the Headmaster's office before opening the door and peeking inside. Everything was quiet, and a very fine layer of dust was starting to cover the room, telling her that likely no one had entered the room since the Headmaster left.

She sighed and closed the door, turning and opening a side door that led to the second floor hallway.

Isabella spent the better part of the next two hours looking through every side room and corner she could think of to try and find where Leo had gone. She asked a few teachers and other staff if they had seen him, but no one had seen him outside of class since lunch.

Growing frustrated, and deciding she needed to get away to clear her thoughts, Isabella left the school and began hiking up a trail along the mountain that led to an overlook of the nearby lake.

The setting sun seemed to pause in the sky as she walked, going down at the same pace she climbed. She passed through a small patch of pine trees that clung to the mountainside and then stepped out onto a span of stone that jutted out from the mountain over the small lake below.

Isabella scanned everything below her. The lake, the training fields, and the school all seemed far away below her. She took a deep breath, closing her eyes, feeling the last rays of the day's sun landing on her.

"So you did leave the school grounds this late in the day. I thought someone like you would respect the school rules more."

Isabella's fists clenched at her sides and her teeth ground together as she heard Titus's voice.

"I certainly hope you didn't follow me out here to whine about rules." Isabella responded, turning around sharply to face Titus, who was still standing just outside the treeline.

"No, I came out to make my proposition."

It took every fiber of self control for Isabella not to growl angrily.

"And I already told you I wasn't interested, and I have had a very long day. So choose your next words carefully, we are a long way from the school, and I am losing patience."

Titus scowled.

"I'm offering you a chance to gain privilege and political power. You mentioned ruling the world before. What I am offering is not far off."

Isabella frowned, not liking a word Titus was saying.

"I don't want power. I don't want privilege. What I want is for you to leave me alone. I have more important things to worry about right now."

Titus took a step forward.

"But if you joined my family there would be nothing left for you to worry about anymore."

Isabella froze, taken aback by what she had just heard. Titus stood, quietly, sure that what he had just said made all the sense in the world.

"Do you realize who you are talking to?" Isabella asked, an angry fire lighting in her chest and a faint red aura settling around her shoulders. "One of the people you try to torment on a daily basis. The friend of the person you do everything in your power to make feel worthless. Why would I ever agree to go with you anywhere!?" As she spoke her voice rose and rose until she was screaming loud enough to hear her voice echoing off the mountains.

"Because you are the only choice worthy of a King!" Titus shouted back. Isabella felt a shock travel through her at this admission.

"We are not to discuss our cards while we still attend this school." Called a voice from behind Titus.

Isabella felt another shock, and Titus whirled around to face Leo as he made his way up the path.

"What are the two of you doing up here this late?" Leo asked before shaking his head. "No, never mind. It's not safe here. Both of you need to go back to the school immediately." Isabella could see that the normally easygoing Leo was deadly serious as he passed Titus and made his way towards her.

"This has nothing to do with you." Titus spat. "This discussion is between me and Isabella."

Leo paused, his face clearly showing his growing impatience. He turned around and faced Titus.

"Indeed. But it also seems loud and clear that Isabella has made her choice. Neither you, nor I, have the right to make her change that decision."

Isabella felt her throat grow tight with concern when Leo used her full name.

"Now I will warn you once again, It is not safe here. You need to leave." Rage was growing on Titus's face.

"I am tired of you acting like you are so much better than me Leo, I am going beat that smug attitude out of you if it's the last thing I do."

Titus half turned and lowered himself into a fighting stance.

"It will be if you try to cast magic here." Leo warned. "The Leylines that normally flow beneath the school have shifted. They are sitting dangerously close to each other below us. If you use magic now, you could pull them together in opposing directions and cause an eruption that could kill all of us and bring down half the mountain."

Isabella slowly realized what Leo had been doing over the last two days, and it was because of this that she only half heard Titus shouting back at Leo.

"Do you think I'm stupid? Who would believe that? It's obvious you're jealous that I got to her first and you're trying to muscle your way in." Titus was fuming, and his face was turning dark red.

"What I feel towards Isabella doesn't matter. Only she can choose who she wants to spend her time with. If you want to fight over it I will gladly defend her. You just choose a time and I will be there. But not here. Not now."

Isabella shook herself as she heard Leo speak, a strange feeling between happiness and fear washing over her.

Titus was shaking now. Leo growled.

"It. Is. Not! Safe!! Here!!!" Leo shouted forcefully, putting growing emphasis on each word. Isabella felt herself trembling. In all their years at The Academy she had never once heard Leo raise his voice like that before.

Titus bared his teeth and raised his arms above his head. A bright blue aura leaped up around him. Leo tried to reach out.

"Don't!" Leo stepped forward, but fire burst around Titus followed by a deafening explosion surrounding them with a blinding light.

Isabella felt herself thrown backwards and then her world went dark.

* * *

Leo felt immense pressure around him, his arms outstretched to either side, extending magic protection around him. He forced his eyes open, checking his surroundings.

Through his protective red aura, Leo could see that the stone beneath their feet had shattered and was slowly being lifted into the air in large chunks.

The flow of magic was so dense it was visible to the naked eye as spindly threads of deep purple and blue energy, twisting around them.

Titus was suspended in a red bubble of power, a look of shock on his face. Leo checked over his shoulder and could see Isabella in a similar bubble, unconscious.

"Thank goodness I caught them in time." Leo thought within himself.

He closed his eyes again and reached out with his senses. He grumbled. The Uinta Line had lifted high enough to run into the Lesser Dragon Line, causing it to split open along it's side.

Leo quickly thought through his options and shook his head,

realizing there was no good option and settling on a plan he wasn't sure he could pull off.

"Titus!" Leo tried to call over the roaring of the raw energy around them. "Can you hear me?"

Titus blinked a few times, slowly looking around until he finally seemed to recognize Leo, then nodded.

"Good." Leo called out. "I think I can close up the split in the Leyline, But I need you to help me cast the spells. Will you work with me and send me all the power you can muster?"

Titus looked around, seeming to realize he was being shielded. He carefully raised himself to his feet and then nodded.

"I'll try." He sounded shaken, and was probably going into shock, but seemed to have enough control of his senses to understand what was happening.

Leo opened his mind and felt Titus timidly reaching out to him. Leo grasped that connection tightly and felt power flowing out of Titus and into him.

Reaching outward again, Leo began grabbing hold of the numerous anchors he had been forging onto both Leylines over the last two days. He took a deep breath then opened his eyes, now glowing red with power, and began reciting a string of invocations.

In his mind he began forging chains, twisting and bending The Uinta Line to bring it in line with the Lesser Dragon Line, and then binding them together along the split with the mental chains.

The flow of power in the Lesser Dragon Line caught hold of the Unita Line and began drawing it into itself. Leo seized the opportunity and poured all of his strength into fusing the two Lines together. Then he felt Titus's power begin to wane.

Leo's eyes flicked over to see him beginning to slump forward against his bubble. Leo quickly released his hold on Titus and felt the full weight of the spells he was still speaking fall on him.

Leo could feel the chains he was binding the Leylines with start to loosen as he struggled to force each word of the spells from his mouth.

In a split second decision, Leo dropped his own magical protections and drew in the raw power flowing around him.

Every ounce of his body erupted in burning agony as the raw energy seared through him, his aura getting swallowed up by it entirely. His voice rose, fighting past the pain to complete the spells, forcing the chains to weave tightly around the two Leylines, pulling them together until the split had fused shut into a new Line.

Feeling his mind starting to fade, Leo called on what strength he had left, a glowing red heart appearing in his left eye.

With one final push, he dragged himself, Titus, and Isabella back onto the remaining part of the trail back that had survived the initial explosion.

As he felt solid ground beneath him again, his power flickered and he collapsed beside the other two, quickly losing consciousness.

* * *

Isabella felt like she had just run a hundred marathons all at once. Everything ached and she could barely even move her fingers at her sides, let alone anything else. On top of that she felt like she was covered, head to toe, in the worst sunburn she had ever had.

As she struggled to remember what had happened she could vaguely hear an argument on the other side of the privacy screen next to her bed.

"I'm trying to tell you that neither of them are in any shape to talk to anyone right now." Isabella recognized Temmy's voice. The voice of a woman she didn't recognize answered.

"I don't care what shape they think they are in, I'm going to give them a piece of my mind for hospitalizing my poor Titus."

Isabella immediately realized it must be Titus's mother on the other side of the screen. She saw Temmy step into view and hold out her arms to block the way. She could also just barely see the head of someone with short, blonde hair standing on the other side of the screen.

"They were hurt just as bad as Titus was, and it wasn't their fault. I'm not going to let you go and yell at them while they are still recovering."

"Get out of my way you nuisance of a child."

Temmy took a half step back and conjured a fiery dart in one hand.

"I won't let you pass." Temmy said nervously.

A laugh, more a cackle, sounded on the other side of the screen.

"You want to start a fight with a real sorceress? With a weak little spell like that? I am going in there, and your little party trick isn't going to stop me."

Temmy scowled angrily and slid her feet together, her right hand extended before her, the fiery dart floating above her pointer and middle fingers. With a wide circular motion, her left hand passed over the dart and around behind her back. The dart split into hundreds of fiery pinpoints of light, spiraling tightly in a cone behind her. A soft yellow aura settled around her shoulders.

"I won't let you pass." Temmy stated again, more firmly.

There was a stunned silence from the other side of the screen for a few moments before the sound of a door opening broke it.

"Miss Artemis, that is completely unnecessary. Please restrain yourself."

Isabella almost sighed in relief when she heard the Headmaster's voice. Temmy quickly brought her hands together and forced them downward, causing all of her darts to evaporate and her aura to disappear.

"And Mrs. Angecles, do please keep your voice down while in the school infirmary." The Headmaster spoke softly, and with seemingly little concern with whom he addressed.

"Headmaster Orpheus. I insist on seeing the students responsible for harming my Son, immediately." Mrs. Angecles demanded, though she did slightly lower the tone of her voice.

"I'm afraid that won't be possible right now, Mrs. Angecles. Neither has woken yet, and it is likely that Leonidas won't wake for some time to come. Besides, no one is responsible for your son's injuries. It was an accident. One that might have been avoided if he had followed school rules and not left school grounds after hours."

Mrs. Angecles sputtered, but the Headmaster continued before she could argue with him.

"Besides, without Leonidas's quick actions it is likely your son wouldn't have survived in the first place. You should be grateful you are here for an injured son, and not for a funeral."

Isabella heard an offended gasp and then stomping and the door slamming shut. Temmy sighed in relief and turned to see Isabella looking at her.

"She's awake." Temmy almost shouted and rushed to Isabella's bedside, grabbing her hand and squeezing it tightly.

"Thanks Temmy." Isabella rasped, only now realizing her throat was dry.

The Headmaster stepped around the privacy screen, his hands clasped in the small of his back. Isabella felt his sharp blue eyes pierce through her like knives.

"I'm sorry, Headmaster." Isabella felt tears welling up in her eyes, but couldn't lift her arm to wipe them away. "I'm so sorry. I didn't know."

The Headmaster sighed, making his way to her side, opposite Temmy. He gently wiped away the tears starting to run down her cheeks then placed his hand on her head.

"Don't be sorry. You couldn't have known what was happening. I told Leo not to say anything to anyone so there wouldn't be a panic. I'm just glad you both made it back."

Isabella sniffled, trying to choke back her tears.

"Is Leo ok?" Isabella saw Temmy look down at the floor and felt her throat tighten, followed by more tears blurring her vision.

"Leo is alive. But he took nearly the full force of the eruption when the Lesser Dragon Line split open. He is severely burned from letting that power flow through him. He will likely never fully recover from the experience, but he should heal in time. At least from his physical injuries."

The Headmaster waited a few moments, letting Isabella absorb the information he had given her. Then he turned to Temmy.

"Miss Artemis, could you please go ask the nurse if she could bring some water for Isabella?"

Temmy nodded and, with another squeeze for Isabella, she turned and quickly left.

Once Temmy was gone, the Headmaster sighed once again, a shudder marring his breath. He carefully brushed Isabella's hair away from her face, and lightly kissed her forehead.

"I felt the whole Dragon Line shudder when it burst." Isabella could see unshed tears glistening in the Headmaster's eyes. "You two are the closest thing to family I have left. In that moment I was afraid I might have lost both of you."

Isabella struggled, trying to reach up and hold his hand, but she was too weak to lift her arm.

"You've raised us since the day we came here." She whispered. "We think of you as family too. You are the closest thing Leo and I will ever have to a father."

The Headmaster smiled sadly, his hand still resting on her head.

"I wish I could have returned sooner. Leo shouldn't have had this responsibility fall to him. But none of the current staff have the power and skill to try and manipulate Leylines quickly, let alone ones as large as these."

Isabella tried to muster a smile.

"It's ok. Leo was happy to do it. I was actually a little upset that he was so willing." Isabella paused for a moment, then spoke again.

"If there ever is something Leo needs to do for you again... Could you let me help him?"

The Headmaster smiled, a knowing and genuine smile that made his eyes sparkle.

"I think I should have from the start."

The Headmaster sighed once more, giving Isabella a light pat on the head before walking towards a door that stood slightly open, opposite the privacy screen where he had entered.

"Get some rest, Isabella. Sleep will be the best thing for your recovery. I promise I will do everything I can to help Leo too."

Isabella tried to nod, all of her muscles screaming at her for doing so.

The Headmaster smiled at her and then slipped through the open door, closing it quietly behind him. He stood silently for several moments before turning to face the single bed in the room.

"I'm sorry Headmaster." Came a quiet and raspy voice from the bed. "I should have handled Titus better."

The Headmaster slowly moved to the bedside, gazing down at Leo.

Leo had two thirds of his body covered in white bandages. His face was uncovered, but there was a square patch of gauze tied over his left eye. He had a blanket covering him from the waist down, and a large clay medallion laying on his bandaged chest, carved with faintly glowing runes.

"Don't blame yourself, Leonidas. Titus is alive because of you."

Leo half chuckled, then coughed with a wince.

"But you are upset with me, aren't you? You wouldn't use my full name otherwise."

The Headmaster smiled sadly.

"I am upset. But not with you, Leo. More upset that I left you in a position where I could have lost you and Isabella."

Leo shook his head slightly, his right eye twitching with discomfort.

"The Leylines would have been fine if I hadn't been so impatient with Titus."

"Anything that happened is due to his poor attitude, not your desire to protect Isabella."

Leo blinked in surprise.

"Did she..." His voice trailed off.

The Headmaster gave him a knowing look.

"Isabella hasn't had the chance to process what happened. With the rupture of the Lesser Dragon Line, she likely won't remember anything you said clearly."

Leo looked away from the Headmaster with a frown.

"I'm not so sure about that." He muttered.

The Headmaster smiled.

"You never let your feelings show, Leo. The chance that she realizes how you feel toward her is slim. As much as it may hurt to hear, she likely doesn't even consider it a possibility."

Leo let out a short laugh, immediately regretting it.

"Fair enough." He said through gritted teeth. "Though, I would be lying if I said I didn't kind of prefer it that way."

The Headmaster carefully placed his hand on Leo's head.

"I know how you feel. You feel like your heart is too fragile to take the blow if she were to reject you. You have given your whole heart to her, and you fear she will leave with it. But you shouldn't worry about things like that. It is in your nature, as King of Hearts, to give your whole heart to everything you do. But it is the curse of Hearts to face inner turmoil and fear of loss. Once you have found your balance, conquered your fears, and allowed yourself to freely feel, you will find that your heart itself will become a bastion from which you can safely uplift the world around you."

Leo felt his heart pounding in his chest, as if to affirm every word the Headmaster spoke. He half chuckled to try and hide it.

"Could I at least wait a few days before having to listen to classroom lectures again?"

The Headmaster laughed.

"Alright then, get some rest." He turned away from the bed, pausing after a couple steps. "Oh, I already spoke with Detective Kardinal. He said he is happy to push back your internship with him another six months so you can recover."

Leo slowly struggled to turn his head.

"Detective Kardinal is still going to let me shadow him? After messing myself up this badly?"

The Headmaster nodded.

"Indeed. If anything, he is more excited to have you after hearing about how you handled the Leyline situation. He wants more people in his agency with expertise in magic and, in his eyes, you have proven you have that expertise."

Leo spent several moments just staring quietly before carefully nodding.

"Thank you for letting me know."

The Headmaster nodded again, this time with a slight smile before he turned away.

"Get some rest Leo. I will have your teachers waive you and Isabella's homework and tests for a while so you can sleep."

"Awesome." Leo said, followed by a very tired sigh of relief.

3

Chapter Three

Leo lowered himself into a leather chair with a grunt. Alexander, a young man with a moderately round stomach, plopped himself in the chair next to him as Detective Kardinal closed the door to his office.

The Detective made his way around to the other side of his desk and sat down, scooting the chair under the desk. He was a fairly average man in all regards. Not very tall, brown hair with streaks of gray, and the beginnings of a beer belly were his most notable features.

"So what did you need us for Detective?" Alexander asked, leaning back comfortably in his chair and lacing his fingers together behind his head of curly black hair.

The Detective looked back and forth between the two of them for a moment before pushing a paper across the desk towards Alexander.

"Firstly, I've approved your request for time off. You're free for the next two weeks."

"Sweet!" Alexander made a little fist pump gesture then leaned forward to grab the paper.

"However, there is also a... sensitive case that has come in as well." The Detective opened a drawer in his desk and pulled out a thick manila envelope, clearly stuffed full of documents and sealed shut with string.

Alexander groaned, looking down sadly at his request form.

"I can take care of that." Leo said. "Alex should still get to take his time off."

Alexander glanced at Leo, and then looked hopefully at the Detective.

The Detective rested his elbows on his desk, his hands gripping tightly together.

"I'm not really comfortable letting you go alone Leo. It looks pretty bad, and I don't have anyone else here at the office who can use magic at the level the two of you can."

Alexander pouted again and leaned back in his chair. Leo glanced between him and the Detective.

"What if I can find someone to go with me?" Leo asked, watching Alexander's eyes widen slightly as he tried not to look hopeful again.

The Detective looked at Leo for a few moments before responding.

"Do you know someone who you could trust to keep confidentiality?"

Leo nodded quickly.

"Of course. A couple people actually and, since I was going home for the weekend anyway, I could get them on board and bring them out when I come back on Monday."

The Detective searched Leo's face for what seemed like ages, then leaned back in his chair.

"Alright. You both have put in a lot of good work over the last fourteen months. I'll let you two work it out. Leo, bring your partner in on Monday and I will have the paperwork for them to sign for the temporary investigation licensing so you can get to work. You can fill Alexander in once he gets back, and then your temp partner can either go home or help finish up the investigation, whatever they want to do."

Alexander did a little dance in his chair.

"Yes! Leo, you are a life saver man."

Leo grinned and gave him a thumbs up.

The Detective took the manila envelope and held it out to Leo.

"Look through it over the weekend. Like I said, it doesn't look good."

"How bad?" Alexander asked, setting his excitement aside and transitioning back into professional mode.

"Provo city has never seen a more blatant use of Outer Magic."

The Detective responded without a moment's hesitation. "Likely more so than anything ever seen in the entire state. The kind of thing that makes people start thinking that Outer Magic is the answer to all their problems, so we need to take care of it."

Leo felt his eyebrows pull together in a frown as he looked down at the envelope in his hands. He could see that Alexander didn't seem much happier about it.

"Just keep your investigation safe, and call in back up from our police contacts if necessary." The Detective said, folding his hands and resting them on his stomach.

"I'll take care of it." Leo said, pushing himself carefully out of his chair, Alexander standing up with him. "We'll go through the channel's we need to to get it done."

The Detective nodded and waved one hand.

"Then have a good weekend. See you back here in a couple weeks Alexander."

Leo and Alexander nodded and then Alexander led the way out of the office. Leo shut the door behind them then slapped Alexander in the shoulder with the manila envelope.

"You didn't tell me you were going on vacation."

Alexander flinched and rubbed his arm where he had gotten hit.

"Well I was going to get around to it eventually."

Leo laughed.

"Before or after you left?"

Alexander sputtered and then blew a raspberry, placing his hand on his chest dramatically.

"Obviously before. I'm not one to just disappear into the night without a word."

"Uh-huh." Leo nodded. "Just like you remembered to let me know that you were going to go off to find lunch while we were searching for what we thought was a chupacabra out by Eagle Mountain?"

"That didn't count." Alexander said, shaking his finger at Leo. "That new sandwich place had just opened up and it needed checking out."

Leo laughed again as they approached their desks.

"I hope you aren't taking two weeks off to go road tripping to sandwich places."

Alexander pulled some papers out of his pocket and tossed them in one of his desk drawers before grabbing his coat from the back of his chair.

"Of course not. I have a legitimate reason for asking for time off. My wife is graduating from the Washington Sorcerer's Academy this week, and I wanted to be there when she did."

Leo paused for a second while slipping into his faded blue trench coat.

"Oh, that's right. I almost forgot you were married."

Alexander gasped, slowly turning to look at Leo, mouth hanging wide open. Leo just scoffed and waved him off.

"You've only mentioned her, like, two times. And you know I'm awful about remembering people. I didn't even remember your name for the first two months we worked together."

"I knew it!" Alexander exclaimed, pointing accusingly at Leo. "I knew it felt like you never called me by name. I just thought you were too wrapped up in yourself to be concerned with other people."

Leo chuckled, shaking his head.

"First off, ouch. I'm not that full of myself. Secondly, for the first week you never stopped talking long enough for me to get a word in edgewise anyway."

Alexander held up his finger and opened his mouth to argue. Then, after a moment of pause, he shrugged and nodded.

"Yeah, that's probably true. But you acted like you were sleepwalking half the time. I had to fill the silence somehow."

Leo shook his head with a smile.

"I was still recovering back then, so I probably was sleepwalking. I should have probably taken more than six months to rest, but I wanted to get to work."

Alexander looked at Leo with one eyebrow raised.

"Are you sure you aren't still recovering? I see you sitting over there at your desk staring off into space all the time."

Leo looked around and then held a finger to his lips.

"Shhh. Nobody is supposed to know about that."

They both laughed and headed out onto the sidewalk, turning towards the parking garage. They walked through the entrance and headed up the stairs to the top level, Leo breathing a bit heavily by the time they reached the top.

"You need more exercise dude." Alexander told him, fishing around in his pockets for his keys.

Leo pulled his own keys out and pushed the button on the remote to unlock his car as he approached.

"But that requires effort, and I'm lazy. Besides, you aren't exactly going to be running any marathons either. It's probably the sandwiches."

Alexander finally managed to find his keys and unlock his car.

"Hey, you leave my sandwiches out of this." Alexander rubbed his belly for emphasis.

Leo chuckled and opened his car door, lowering himself in with an exaggerated groan. Alexander watched him for a moment, his grin slowly fading into a neutral expression.

"Hey. If something comes up with that case, give me a call. I'll come back immediately if you need me to."

Leo shook his head.

"Don't worry about it, Alex. Go celebrate with your wife. Tell her I send my congratulations."

Alexander threw his hands in the air.

"Alright man, I'm going, I'm going." He opened his car door and jumped inside.

"See you in a couple weeks." Leo said, closing his door and giving Alexander a half wave half salute. Alexander returned the gesture before starting his car and backing out of his parking stall.

Leo waited until Alexander was gone, then pulled his seatbelt across his chest with a grunt and started his own car.

"Wonder if Izzy would actually be interested in helping me with the investigation." He said out loud, sitting quietly as his thoughts drifted away for a moment. After a few seconds he shook himself.

"I could always ask Temmy to help me out. I'm sure she wouldn't mind."

Leo put his foot on the break and then reached for the shifter. His hand paused mid way as he remembered a few of the more grisly crime scenes he had helped Detective Kardinal investigate.

"On second thought, maybe I shouldn't ask Temmy." His voice trailed off for a moment before he shook himself once again and shifted the car into gear. He glanced in his rear view mirror and started backing out.

"Maybe I will just hope that Izzy will help me out."

* * *

"Leo!" Isabella shouted down the hall as Leo came into view, climbing the last few steps.

Leo waved with a grin, then made a point to pause at the top of the stairs with his hands on his knees, pretending to be completely winded.

When he straightened up he had about a half second to react before Isabella threw her arms around him.

"Welcome home." Isabella said happily, starting to squeeze him very tightly. "I hate you so much." She said just as happily.

Leo coughed once as Isabella continued to try and crush all the air out of his lungs.

"I'm sorry Izzy, I got really busy." He tried to sound appropriately breathless.

Isabella squeezed a little tighter for a moment and then let go, Leo being sure to gasp dramatically to breathe.

"No calls, no text messages, no emails, not so much as a smoke signal from you in six months." Isabella put her hands on her hips and frowned.

Leo did his best not to grin at her, knowing it would just get him into more trouble.

"I really was busy. I meant to call, but the one time I had the chance it was during your qualifying exams and I didn't want to bother you. How did those go by the way?"

Isabella stuck her nose in the air and turned to head back towards her room.

"I aced them, obviously. I've been doing practical work with the school nurses for the last couple months."

Leo followed her as she spoke, trying to decide how to bring up the subject of work.

"Aced? Well consider me suitably impressed. Congratulations."

Isabella glanced over her shoulder and stared daggers at him through narrowed eyes.

"I don't feel like you are being sincere."

Leo did a double take, putting one hand on his chest and making a face as if he had just been insulted.

"Me? Not sincere? And after I came all this way out just to see you. You wound me, my lady."

Isabella scoffed, though a smile tugged at one corner of her mouth, and stopped in front of her room.

"I hope you will at least come over and say hello to Temmy."

Leo nodded and unlocked his own door.

"I will for sure. I have souvenirs I want to give you guys anyway. Though I have to go have a quick chat with Headmaster Orpheus first."

Leo watched Isabella's eyes light up at the mention of souvenirs, but she quickly turned and opened her door and stepped inside.

"These souvenirs better be good ones then." She said before quickly shutting the door behind her.

Leo chuckled and went into his room, taking his bag off his back and tossing it onto his chair. He could see a thin cloud of dust escape into the air and scrunched his nose.

He rubbed his hands together, then waved his hands face down in front of him. He felt the, now familiar, burning sensation from using magic run through him, and the dust lifted off the surfaces in the room and vanished.

Nodding in satisfaction he turned and left, closing the door behind him. He took two steps, paused for a moment, thinking of the envelope in his bag. He took two steps backwards and locked his door, then continued down the hall until he reached the Headmaster's office.

He knocked twice then opened the door.

"Come in Leo, I'm just filling out some paperwork." The Headmaster sat at his desk, a long feather quill in his hand that twitched back and forth as he wrote.

Leo closed the door behind him and made his way to the chair opposite The Headmaster, lowering himself into it with a grunt.

"How have you been feeling?" The Headmaster asked, his eyes moving smoothly back and forth between books and notes scattered on his desk.

Leo shrugged.

"Pretty good I guess. Most days I don't feel too sore."

The Headmaster nodded, shuffling some papers around before continuing to write.

"And how about when you use magic?"

Leo looked down at his hands, opening and closing them a few times.

"Minor magic isn't bad anymore. Feels a bit like brushing up against a mostly healed sunburn. Higher magic burns some, but I think I'm mostly used to it and it kind of just feels normal now. Though, I would probably be a bit afraid of trying anything too advanced just yet."

The Headmaster chuckled, a half smile on his face as he set down his quill.

"As long as you are using your magic consistently the sensitivity should get better." The Headmaster's piercing blue eyes seemed to stare straight through Leo. "As long as you don't try drawing in any natural energy without thoroughly mixing it with your own power first. Your channels are still raw and will likely still need a few more years to heal entirely."

Leo nodded with a grin.

"Oh I don't plan on playing with natural energy ever again if I can help it."

The Headmaster leaned forward, resting his elbows on his desk and folding his hands together.

"How have things been, Leo?"

Leo leaned back against the chair and laid his head back with a groan.

"It's been sooo busy." He grumbled. "There is so much to do. We had to find a kid who chased off after some will o' the wisps. Went searching for a chupacabra, which just turned out to be a lost great dane. Some lady managed to accidentally trap a half dozen angry spirits in her house because she tried to curse her neighbor for putting his Christmas decorations up a month early, but she had no idea what she was doing and messed up and ended up cursing herself instead."

The Headmaster laughed, hiding his face behind his hands and shaking his head. Leo sat up straight again.

"Right? Like, there are so many public service things telling people not to mess with magic if they haven't been trained. But then people just default to Witchcraft or Vodou or weird DIY rituals, which are the absolute worst for the untrained and are so easy to mess up it's not even funny."

Leo took a deep breath and sighed.

"I guess I should just be glad that Detective Kardinal doesn't give me all the domestic stuff a lot of the other junior detectives have to deal with. I would go insane if I had to sit outside some random guy's house for sixteen hours watching him because his wife thinks he's cheating or something."

The Headmaster nodded.

"Indeed. Though, a case like that might be preferable to something terrible."

Leo nodded slowly.

"True enough. I've had one or two now that made it hard to eat for a while." Leo stared into space for a moment before something clicked in his brain.

"Oh! I almost forgot. I was going to ask if it would be possible for me to steal Izzy for a couple weeks."

The Headmaster laughed.

"I don't know how much Isabella would appreciate getting kidnapped."

Leo scratched his chin for a few seconds.

"Ok, so I will probably have to convince her to steal herself, but I mean after that part. I need a partner for a couple weeks since my normal partner is out of town and there is an important case we were given."

The Headmaster leaned back in his chair.

"Detective Kardinal still wants it investigated? Can't it wait until your partner gets back?"

Leo glanced over his shoulder to make sure he had closed the door on his way in, then leaned forward and rested his elbows on his knees.

"I haven't had a chance to look at the file yet, but I was told it is one of the biggest instances of Outer Magic ever seen in the area. With the level of urgency the Detective put on it, I imagine it is likely an ongoing curse or ritual that needs to be taken apart by someone who knows how to do it safely."

Leo kept his voice low, even though he knew there was little chance of being overheard.

"My partner offered to stay, but his wife is graduating from a branch of The Academy out of state, and I didn't think he should miss something like that. I convinced Detective Kardinal to let him go, but I have to find a capable partner to cover the two weeks until he gets back. I thought I would ask Izzy or Temmy to help me out, But I would rather not ask Temmy just in case it is awful."

"But you are ok with asking Isabella?"

Leo rubbed his forehead a few times.

"I don't really want to expose Izzy to anything awful either, but I think she would be able to keep herself together if it is awful. Plus, she has the kind of expertise she would need to help me if it is a curse that needs to be unraveled."

The Headmaster nodded slowly.

"Well, all of this hinges on whether or not Isabella would agree to go with you. However, if she does agree, I am willing to sign off on her leave from training with the infirmary staff."

Leo leaned back in his chair, letting out a genuine sigh of relief.

"Oh good. That's one worry off my shoulders. Now I just have to convince Izzy." He paused for a few seconds. "Actually, maybe that's more worrying."

The Headmaster chuckled, reaching down and picking up his quill again.

"Well, only one thing that can be done about that."

Leo forced himself out of his chair with a groan.

"I guess. Please come save me if she lights me on fire or something."

"I'm sure she won't light you on fire if you ask nicely."

Leo shrugged, then said goodbye and left the office. He made his way back to his room and unlocked the door, stepping inside briefly to grab two small boxes out of his bag before locking his door again and stepping across the hall.

He carefully knocked on the door and, a few moments later, Isabella opened it.

"I come bearing gifts." Leo said, holding out the small boxes.

Isabella looked at the boxes skeptically then looked over her shoulder.

"I don't know Temmy, they look pretty small. Should I let him in?"

Leo heard a quiet reply, but couldn't quite make out what was said. Isabella looked back at him, like she wasn't sure whether to let him in or not, but eventually stepped back and swung the door open for him.

"Alright, I guess we will accept your gifts then."

Leo bowed dramatically.

"I thank you for your gracious hospitality." He said, walking inside and sidestepping to avoid getting slapped by Isabella.

Temmy was sitting at their small dining table, typing on a relatively new looking laptop. Leo walked in and placed one of the boxes next to her.

"Greetings Temmy, fantastic to see you, how have you been?"

Temmy typed a few more words and then closed the laptop.

"I have been fine, thank you. You didn't have to bring me anything though." She looked down at the box beside her.

Leo scoffed.

"Of course I was going to bring you something. Why would I not?" He turned as Isabella followed him into the room and he held out the second box.

"Peace offerings, please don't hurt me."

Isabella accepted the box and untied the string holding it shut.

"I'll decide after I see what it is."

Leo grinned, but took a half step away just in case.

Isabella lifted the top of the box away and pulled aside a piece of brown paper to reveal a small crystal ball sitting on a polished brass base. Temmy opened her own box to reveal a similar crystal.

Isabella glanced up at Leo with one eyebrow raised. He quickly ducked behind the chair Temmy was sitting on.

"I promise, it's really cool." He said, peeking up from around Temmy's shoulder.

Isabella carefully pulled the crystal and stand out of the box and looked back and forth between it and Leo.

"How so?" She asked, clearly not convinced.

Leo waited until Temmy had pulled hers out of the box and sat it on the table, then carefully reached around and placed one finger on top of the crystal.

Immediately a glowing, liquid red smoke seemed to pour out of his finger into the crystal. The smoke swirled around and changed colors from red to green and then to blue.

Isabella's eyes widened.

"Wait! How?" She exclaimed, taking a step towards the table.

Leo quickly let go of the crystal and hid behind Temmy again. The crystal swirled and then quickly became clear.

Isabella put her crystal on the table and put a finger on top of it, but nothing happened.

"How did you make it do that?" She asked, looking over at Leo.

Leo slowly got a wolfish grin on his face then cupped his hand next to Temmy's ear and whispered something to her. Temmy nodded a few times, then half turned her head to look at him. He just motioned towards the crystal with one hand and nodded back.

Temmy tentatively reached out and put one finger on top of the crystal. After a moment, a silky smooth trail of pink smoke wound its way from Temmy's finger, down the sides of the crystal, in lazy spirals.

Isabella blinked a few times and then pouted.

"How come I can't do it?"

Leo finally stood up and made his way around Temmy's chair to stand next to Isabella.

"Do you want to know the secret?"

Isabella looked at him with a scowl, and Leo tried not to laugh. Even Temmy started to smile.

Leo reached out and placed his finger over the top of Isabella's. She immediately felt power flow from his finger into hers, then drain away into the crystal. The crystal was suddenly filled with little dancing lights that trailed red and pink smoke behind them.

"These little crystal balls are made the same way the Pylon in the Academy's North Tower was made. That means they resonate the same way the Pylon does when you apply magic to it. It isn't as powerful, of course, but it can make really cool patterns depending on how you channel your power into it."

Leo lifted his finger away, and Isabella poured her own power into the crystal. The dancing lights turned gold and spun in a little circle, leaving trails in the silky smoke.

"That's so cool." Isabella said absently before catching herself and clearing her throat.

"I mean, I guess this is an acceptable gift."

Temmy nodded and now fully smiled.

"Yes, thank you very much. I think they are beautiful."

Leo grinned and looked at Isabella.

Isabella wanted to frown, but she felt her lips smiling when she looked at Temmy.

"Oh all right, they are awesome and I love it. There, are you happy?"

Leo nodded, still grinning.

"Very much so."

Isabella sighed and turned to go into the kitchenette.

"Well, we are about to have dinner, so you might as well stay and have some food."

Leo bowed.

"You are far too kind."

"I know." Isabella said, trying to sound exasperated.

Leo stood around for several moments, then decided to walk over to stand beside Isabella as she started to cook.

"Hey Izzy, um, could I ask you for a favor? After dinner I mean."

Isabella pulled a bowl out of one of the cupboards and put it on the counter. She glanced over her shoulder to answer, but was caught off guard by Leo's unusually serious face.

She fully turned to face him and he looked her in the eye, without looking away like he had been since their accident on the mountain.

"What kind of favor?" She asked, now starting to worry.

Leo continued to look her in the eyes for several moments, seeming to be searching for something. Eventually he just kind of waved with one hand and half turned away.

"I'll ask after dinner. I don't want to bother you with it while you are trying to cook."

Isabella resisted the urge to frown, and opted to try and distract Leo from whatever weight he seemed to be carrying. She opened a drawer and pulled out a wooden spoon, which she immediately turned and smacked him with.

"Well then get out of my kitchen so I can cook. You will just get in my way, and at the very least I don't want to keep Temmy waiting."

Leo gasped loudly.

"Oh no! You're right! I'm so sorry Temmy!"

Temmy blinked a few times in surprise.

"I...It's ok. There isn't any hurry."

Isabella nodded.

"Yep, you heard her. She's starving and can't wait another moment, so out of the way."

Isabella swiped at Leo again with the spoon.

"N...no, I'm really..." Temmy tried to speak, but Leo jumped out of reach of the spoon and interrupted.

"Poor Temmy! I have wronged such a paragon of greatness."

Leo rushed to the dining table, placing his clasped hands on top, and bowed his head as deeply as he could manage.

"Please forgive me. The great Goddess of the Kitchen has shown me the error of my ways."

"Don't do it Temmy." Isabella called from the kitchenette, cracking an egg into her bowl, trying not to laugh.

"Um, it's ok." Temmy said, slightly confused as to what was going on. "You don't need to apologize."

Leo's head shot up.

"Such benevolence. Such kindness. I promise I shall use this opportunity to better myself, Great Temmy."

Leo ducked as the wooden spoon flew across the room at him.

"You shush." Isabella said, her cheeks turning red from trying not to laugh.

Leo stood up straight, making a zipping motion across his mouth then placing one hand over his heart. He stood silently at attention for several moments.

Temmy sat quietly for a moment, looking back and forth between Leo and Isabella, still not sure what was going on, but having a hard time not having a smile creep onto her face.

She gathered her laptop and crystal and sat them on another chair across the room, then grabbed a deck of cards and returned to the table.

"Do you want to play a game while we wait?" She asked Leo, opening the cards to shuffle them.

Leo opened his mouth to speak, then glanced at Isabella and made the zipping motion over his lips again before giving Temmy a thumbs up and sitting at the table to wait for dinner.

4

Chapter Four

Isabella sat in the passenger seat of Leo's car, slowly turning her new metal detective badge over in her hands. It was a simple polished relief of Detective Kardinal's company crest, a dragonscale shield, with a complex rune system carved into the back.

Leo pulled a large manila envelope from the center console and handed it to Isabella while they waited for their light to turn green.

"Now that you have your temp license, you can actually look at what we are investigating."

Isabella took the envelope and opened it, pulling out the stack of papers inside.

"The first few pages are the pictures and a basic description, that will give you an idea of what we are looking at. The rest are initial observations police made, but that won't be as important, since we are just going to go make our own observations right now."

Leo pulled out onto university avenue and headed south, and Isabella shuffled through a couple papers. Most of the pictures were grainy and zoomed in to the point of being almost useless.

"These are really hard to see." Isabella said, tilting her head to one side. "and what I can see doesn't really seem to make much sense."

Leo nodded as he checked over one shoulder and signaled to change lanes.

"That's why they hired Detective Kardinal to investigate in the first place. Police said it didn't make a lot of sense to them. And the pictures are bad on purpose. Some magic is based in shapes and symbolism like runes are, and that can transfer through pictures. They don't want to accidentally transfer a curse to someone because they were carrying too clear of a picture of the wrong things."

Isabella nodded her understanding and flipped another page to skim over the description of the site.

"Altar, covered in a burgundy velvet material, two off white candles and wooden bowl with unknown remains on altar. Pillar behind altar decorated with several flowering tree branches and the bare skull of a member of the Cervidae family. Circle of salt laid out in front of the altar, a small pile of ash at its center, and circle surrounded by various remnants of materials thought to be used in original ritual." Isabella scrunched her nose.

"That doesn't seem right. Any one of those things on their own might make sense, but all at once in the same place?"

Leo opened his mouth to answer, then grunted and swerved slightly as a small green car cut in front of him to make a turn at the last second.

"Learn to signal!" Leo complained at the car, before moving into the turn lane at the next light and heading towards the mountains.

"Yeah, they aren't sure whether these were different things that just happened in the same place, or if someone tried to make up something using a bunch of different disciplines. There was magic present at the site when it was discovered so something was happening, we just have to try and figure out what it was, and if it was all tied together or not."

Isabella slowly nodded her understanding and continued to read through the more detailed observations from the various officers. After a few minutes she felt the car slow to a stop and Leo put the car into park and shut off the engine.

Isabella looked up and found they had parked in front of a small warehouse surrounded by a yellow police tape line.

Leo got out and Isabella followed him, leaving the police report on her seat. Leo led the way to the police line and lifted the tape for Isabella to go under, holding up his badge in one hand.

"Make sure you have your badge in hand as you go through. The police put up a barrier to preserve the scene and our badges are our key inside."

Isabella nodded, and slipped under the tape, holding her badge out in front of her. As she passed under the tape the runes on the back of her badge started glowing and she felt as if she passed through a thin curtain.

Leo followed behind, waving his badge in front of him as if brushing past something, then led the way to the front door of the warehouse. He used a small key to unlock the door, then held the door open for Isabella to go inside.

Inside they found a large open space, supported by large wooden pillars that ran down the center of the building. The ritual site sat against the central pillars, with several pallets of assorted boxes haphazardly shoved aside to make room for it.

Leo walked around the pallets and stood at the edge of the circle of salt. Isabella followed carefully behind, looking around the room, unsure of what she needed to do.

As she walked, Isabella suddenly felt something wash over her that made her stomach tighten, and almost felt like she could smell something off for a fleeting moment.

"There is definitely still magic flowing through the ritual, which is weird since the police barrier should essentially be halting the passage of time for the individual parts."

Isabella frowned and scanned over everything with her eyes pausing on the altar.

"If it is a curse, and it was already established by the time the ritual was found and the police sealed it off, then the person it is connected to outside the barrier could be drawing the power through the system without the barrier having any real effect."

Leo nodded his agreement, holding out one hand and releasing a trickle of energy.

"Salt has no power in it. Whatever the original purpose the circle had, it seems that purpose was fulfilled." As he spoke he used his foot to push some salt aside to make a gap in the circle.

Leo stepped carefully inside the circle and squatted down next to the pile of ash in its center. Reaching out he stirred the pile around with one finger then rubbed the residue between his finger and thumb.

"Some kind of paper ash. Though it seems like a lot of ash. I wouldn't usually expect so much paper to be involved with most magic."

Isabella carefully stepped around the side of the circle to get a better look.

"If it is an active curse, maybe it was the name and personal information of the one being cursed? Though if it was a lot of paper being burned maybe it was for many targets. If it wasn't directly related to the curse, perhaps it was the written contract that a spirit was meant to agree to, and it burned after the agreement was made."

Leo glanced over his shoulder at Isabella and she felt her cheeks burn a bit, feeling self conscious about putting out suggestions.

"Izzy... You are absolutely brilliant."

Isabella blinked a few times in surprise as Leo stood with a grunt and pulled a small notebook and pen out of his coat pocket.

"Multiple targets or spiritual contract. Could also be a type of Tao curse if the practitioner was not particularly skilled and needed multiple paper talismans to make the curse successful, though that also seems unlikely since usually paper tags need to remain whole. Though if not a curse, could still be a spiritual contract. Also entirely possible that the ash is just the consequence of burning something that they didn't want anyone to find and, since the circle of salt was done being used, the center of the circle was just the most convenient place to burn whatever it was."

Leo jotted down his notes as he spoke, occasionally glancing over his notepad too look at the stuff around him. After several moments of note taking, he put the notebook and pen back in his pocket and stepped over to the altar.

Isabella followed him, being careful not to step on any of the debris around the site.

Leo leaned down and placed one hand against the side of the large concrete block that made up the makeshift altar.

"Altar is cold." He observed. "The candles are sitting in small brass candle-holders, but don't seem to have ever been lit." His hand moved to the velvety cloth that was draped over the center of the altar.

"Very soft altar cloth, possibly velvet, red-brown in color. Doesn't seem likely that the color or material has any significance to the magic being used, so probably just an altar cloth."

Isabella watched Leo cast an expert eye over everything as he moved his hand to the wooden bowl in the center. He carefully lifted one edge, leaning over further to see under it.

"Bowl seems carved at first glance, but looks to be mass manufactured to appear as such."

Leo carefully let go of the bowl and reached into his pocket, taking out a pair of latex gloves and putting them on before reaching into the bowl and carefully removing a small animal bone. He twisted it around in his fingers, looking at all sides of the bone before laying it back in the bowl. He straightened up and removed his gloves.

"Looks like rabbit bones most likely, though there is no skull and it doesn't look like the rest of the skeleton is complete either. Not sure if it was meant as a sacrifice of some sort, or if the parts of the animal were used as a reagent for something."

"That's awful, poor thing." Isabella frowned, and Leo half smiled in a way that said he agreed with her.

"Unfortunately a lot of people who were never trained in magic feel like some sort of sacrifice is necessary, even if the ritual they are following doesn't call for it. They are just convinced that curses require something more. On the other hand, some practices do use animal parts as reagents so it's hard to tell right out of the gate."

Leo turned around and faced the altar again, this time looking up at the decorated pillar behind it.

"Deer skull, male with small antlers, tree branches from a couple different trees." Leo walked all the way around the pillar and back to the front of the altar.

"Everything tied to the pillar with some sort of rough woven rope, but otherwise very simply organized."

Isabella stepped around the side of the pillar and looked more closely at the tree branches.

"Peach, cherry, and I think the third one is plum?" She said, as if she was asking herself if she was sure. Leo took out his notebook and jotted it down, then looked back up at the deer skull.

"Two points either side, probably not important but, worth writing down anyway." He slowly turned, looking at the site as a whole.

"So what do you think?" He asked, looking back to Isabella.

Isabella also took a moment to look around before answering.

"I'm not sure. I sense magic in the air, but it doesn't actually seem to be affixed to anything, so I don't know what it is meant to be doing. And everything in the room seems weirdly deliberate. Like it was very carefully planned out, even though none of it seems connected. Even the clutter and the warehouse goods that were pushed out of the way almost seem like their positions were not an accident."

Leo listened intently as Isabella spoke, his eyes following her words around the room. He nodded carefully as she finished, lifting his notebook again and sketching out the rough layout of the site, clutter and other things included.

"You are right, it feels like this was done meticulously." Leo said as he sketched. "Though the magic isn't tied to the site, so I think it will be safe to tell the police that they can come in and clean everything up and put it into evidence. Though I do want to go have a word with a couple of people before we do, just to be safe."

Isabella nodded slowly, watching Leo work, and trying to think of something to say so she didn't have to stand around awkwardly in the silence while he was busy.

"Who do we need to talk to?" She finally asked, and Leo flipped his notebook shut and slid it back into his pocket.

"I know a guy who could help us track down anything in here we might have missed. And if it is a curse, he could also find the victim or victims which could help us find who cast it in the first place. The second person I want to speak to is a wizard, who is a practicing Wiccan, who leads a circle in the area. The ritual here doesn't exactly seem Wiccan in origin I don't think, but I'm not really an expert in Wicca so I want to check to be sure."

Isabella nodded and Leo turned and grinned at her.

"You made some great observations though Izzy, I'm glad you agreed to come along and help me out."

Isabella pushed some of her hair out of her face, turning to look at the rest of the room again as she felt her cheeks burn slightly.

"Well you said it was a pretty big problem, so I didn't want to just ignore it if I could do something about it." She felt like she was making excuses rather than giving an explanation.

Leo's grin widened and he half turned, waving for her to lead the way out.

"Well I, for one, am glad you came. Usually sites like this are small and the casters try to hide them. Something this large and out in the open was something I wasn't looking forward to investigating, especially if I had to come check it out alone."

Isabella squared her shoulders and lead the way out of the warehouse confidently, careful not to step on anything on the way out.

"Then you should be grateful I graced you with my presence, and you should buy me lunch."

Leo laughed, closing and locking the warehouse door as they left.

"Alright, you got me. We will stop for some food on the way to visit our first guy. I know a place that has pretty good sandwiches."

* * *

Isabella stared openly at the large, Victorian style mansion as Leo pulled into the large circular drive, the last few bites of her sandwich left forgotten in her hands. They parked and Leo shut off the car and then grinned at Isabella.

"I have a cooler in the back if you want to save the rest for later." He said, pointing at what remained of the sandwich.

Isabella absently wrapped up the sandwich and handed it to Leo, watching as several gardeners came around the side of the house to start taking care of the flower beds along the front.

"What do we need to do here?" Isabella asked, opening her door to get out as Leo lifted himself out of the car with a grunt.

"The guy I told you about, the one who could help us go over the site one more time and find any potential victims? He lives here." Leo popped the trunk of his car and put Isabella's sandwich in a red plastic cooler as he spoke.

"Also, one of Headmaster Orpheus's friends also lives here, so I figured we could say hello."

Isabella blinked, trying to look back at Leo but having a hard time looking away from the, almost glittering, mansion.

Before she could ask Leo any of the questions swimming around in her head, however, a maid with long black hair and round glasses approached Isabella.

"How are you this morning? What brings you to Koyane Manor?"

Isabella stood silently, trying to figure out what to say. Leo slammed the trunk shut and waved.

"Hey Tanya, we just came to see Conner, if he is around. And we figured we would pay our respects to Master Shepherd if he has a spare moment."

The maid's eyes lit up at the sight of Leo and she quickly bowed.

"Welcome back Master Leo, it is good to see you again." Isabella finally glanced back over her shoulder at Leo as he joined her.

"Master Leo?" Isabella asked incredulously, feeling one of her eyebrows rising slightly.

Leo shrugged.

"They are big on formality here." He turned back to the maid as she stood straight again.

"This is my friend Isabella. She is helping me out today and I figured it would be good to introduce her to Master Shepherd so we could give him Headmaster Orpheus's regards."

The maid nodded with a smile and waved towards the front entrance.

"Please follow me."

She turned and headed inside, Leo and Isabella following along behind her. They walked through a large foyer and down a hallway to a sitting room and the maid waved to indicate the room.

"Please make yourselves comfortable and I will let Master Shepherd know you are here. I will also send someone to fetch Conner for you. Would you like any refreshment while you wait?"

Leo shook his head with a chuckle.

"We just ate, but thank you anyway Tanya. And you don't need to stand on ceremony so much. We aren't fancy guests or anything."

The maid smiled brightly with her hands clasped at her waist.

"You will always be treated as royalty here, Master Leo. If you, or Lady Isabella, have need of anything, please do not hesitate to ask." With another bow she quickly drifted out of the room.

Leo nudged Isabella and pointed at some arm chairs placed around a crystal glass coffee table.

"She did say make yourself comfortable, Lady Izzy." Isabella scowled at Leo as she shook herself out of her initial culture shock.

"How are you supposed to be comfortable in such a large fancy mansion?" She asked, moving over and carefully sitting down on the edge of one of the chairs.

Leo laughed and sat down in the chair next to her, lowering himself down using the armrests with a fleeting look of discomfort crossing his face as he did.

"You live in a literal castle Izzy. Why should a mansion be so intimidating?"

Isabella stuck her nose in the air importantly, realizing that The Academy really was nothing short of a castle.

"I suppose that's true. I guess you will have to start treating me like a queen."

Leo scratched his chin, as if thinking deeply on something.

"Queen Izzy. I guess that makes Temmy Princess Temmy. And I would be..."

"The Court Jester." Isabella said, without a moment's hesitation.

Leo pouted.

"Can I at least be a Baron? Or maybe a Marquis? Oh, a Viscount perhaps?"

Isabella shook her head.

"Nope, you are definitely Court Jester material."

Leo scratched the back of his head for a moment.

"Well, I guess I am pretty hilarious."

Isabella opened her mouth to speak, but a muffled voice beat her to it.

"You only think you are hilarious. Your humor is mediocre at best."

Leo grinned, and pushed himself out of his chair with a grunt.

"So rude. Help a guy out here Conner, I'm trying to get a promotion."

Leo walked across the room to the doorway to meet a tall, thin man wearing an almost futuristic looking face mask that covered his mouth and nose. It had a clasp on one side of his face that seemed to allow the mask to open.

They shook hands and the man wearing the mask shook his head.

"Just calling it like I see it. Trying to save this poor girl from hiring a bad jester."

Isabella stood trying to hide her growing smile.

Leo gestured to Isabella.

"This is Isabella, a good friend of mine and my partner for the time being until Alex gets back from his vacation. Izzy, this is Conner. A friend of Detective Kardinal who helps us out on cases occasionally."

Isabella and Conner shook hands.

"Pleasure to meet you My Lady. I am sorry you have to spend your time with this poor excuse for a detective."

Leo pouted again and Isabella did her best not to laugh at him.

"And a pleasure to meet you Conner. Don't worry, I grew up having to deal with him. I can handle it."

Leo grumbled, but made his way back to his chair. As he got there, he immediately turned around and pulled his notebook out of his pocket.

"Probably should let you look at this before I sit down again." He said, walking back over and handing the notebook to Conner. "Since we sadly didn't come all this way just to chat."

Conner took the notebook and looked through the pages as Leo went and sat back down. After a few moments he looked up at Leo.

"This is a pretty dramatic ritual site. I hadn't heard about anything this size going on."

Leo nodded.

"Police caught it pretty quick and sealed it off. They didn't want people to start panicking over it. Only the warehouse manager who called the police even saw what was in there."

Conner nodded, moving to sit in one of the chairs across from Leo, and continued flipping through the notebook. Isabella also returned to her chair and sat down, waiting to see what else Conner had to say.

After several minutes of silence Conner leaned back in his chair.

"Not a whole lot to go off of, is there?"

Leo shook his head.

"Lots of stuff, almost none of it useful. Whoever did it was either an idiot who had no idea what they were doing, or a master who knew how to hide everything they were doing. That's why I was hoping you wouldn't mind going down and taking a look around before I gave the police the all clear to clean up the site."

Conner nodded, closing the notebook and tossing it over to Leo.

"Yeah, I can go take a look. Which officers went in?"

Leo tilted his head back and stared off into the corner of the room for a second.

"Richter, Polland, and..." He trailed off, trying to remember the last name.

"Dunnam, was the name I saw I think." Isabella offered.

Leo snapped his fingers.

"Dunnam! That's right. I kept thinking of his stupid looking villain mustache and couldn't remember his name."

Conner chuckled.

"Dunnam is rather proud of that mustache of his. So just old boys then. That makes it easier, won't have to pick out scents for the newer officers. So just them and the two of you then?"

Leo nodded.

"Probably some left over smells from the warehouse workers, but we should be the only ones who went in the warehouse after the ritual was completed."

Isabella was suddenly finding it hard to follow the conversation. Conner stood and made his way around the coffee table to her side and got down on one knee next to her.

"I know this is going to sound weird, so I apologize, But may I smell your hair miss?"

Isabella blinked, noticing out of the corner of her eye that Leo was grinning and trying not to laugh.

"Um, I..." Isabella fumbled over finding a response, and Leo finally got himself under control enough to speak.

"What do they call you guys these days Conner? I know some people were getting upset over some names being insensitive or something."

Conner shook his head with an unenthusiastic laugh.

"Those people are idiots, and most of them aren't even Aspects in the first place."

Isabella had something click in her brain at the mention of Aspects, and Leo spoke to confirm it.

"He is a Dog Aspect, Izzy. That's how he helps us out, by tracking the scent of the people involved. He can even track the smell of specific people's magic. He said it in a way that makes him sound creepy, but he really just needs to get your scent so he can pick it out of the other smells at the warehouse and ignore it."

Isabella shook herself in surprise and suddenly Conner's mask made sense to her.

"Oh, you are an Animal Aspect, and a Zodiac Aspect at that. That makes a lot of sense now. I am sorry, I was just surprised when you asked and didn't know how to respond. It's alright with me if you need to smell my hair."

Isabella pulled her ponytail from behind her and laid it over her shoulder so it would be easier to get to. Conner nodded, unclasping his mask on one side and swinging it out of the way, revealing a slim, clean shaven face.

Conner carefully lifted the end of Isabella's ponytail and held it a few inches away from his nose. He took a long inhale through his nose and then dropped her hair and closed his mask before exhaling. He sat quietly for a few moments with his eyes closed, then stood up.

"Thank you Miss, I understand it can be an uncomfortable thing for someone to smell you, so I hope I didn't cause too much of a problem for you."

Isabella shook her head and smiled politely.

"Not at all. I understand why you needed to, and I showered this morning so I would hope I didn't smell bad."

Conner laughed.

"You smell much better than a lot of people I've smelled. You smell better than Leo at the very least."

"Hey!" Leo complained. "I showered this morning too."

Conner scoffed.

"You smell burnt and like off brand soap. She smells like lavender and mountain air."

Leo opened his mouth to complain, but after a few moments of thought he nodded.

"Ok, you know what? That makes a lot of sense. Fair enough. I like the smell of my soap though."

Isabella resisted the urge to say something sarcastic and instead fixed her hair. Conner shrugged and turned towards the door.

"Also should let you know that Miss Tanya is on her way down the stairs with Master Shepherd, so they should be here in a minute."

Leo saluted and then waved at Conner.

"Thanks Conner, let me know if you find anything else or if I can give the police the ok to clean up."

Conner waved behind him without turning.

"Will do."

He stepped out the door, waiting for a moment before bowing to someone in the hall, and then left. A moment later Tanya appeared in the doorway, motioning through with one hand.

A tall, thin man with dark brown hair and bright brown eyes entered the room. He was wearing a set of unassuming, sleek black clothes, similar to the butlers who roamed the halls of the mansion, but carried with him the air of someone far more important than a simple servant.

Leo quickly struggled to his feet and bowed slightly, Isabella following suit.

"Master Shepherd, it is good to see you again. Headmaster Orpheus sends his regards."

The man smiled with a nod.

"Good morning, Leonidas. Please, have a seat. No need for you to treat me any differently than you do Orpheus."

Leo chuckled but waved to Isabella before sitting down.

"This is Isabella. Since we were going to be stopping by here anyway, I wanted to bring her to meet you."

Master Shepherd smiled at her, placing one arm across his chest and bowing to her, a gesture she quickly returned.

"Miss Isabella, I am glad to finally meet you in person. Orpheus speaks fondly of you, and Leonidas holds you in high regard. Everyone calls me Master Shepherd, so you may as well do the same."

"A pleasure to meet you Master Shepherd. Headmaster Orpheus has great respect for you, and I am also glad to finally meet you in person. Though I am sure whatever he has said of me is a gross exaggeration."

Master Shepherd made his way to a chair and sat, Tanya following close at hand.

"Orpheus is a sentimental man, but not one prone to exaggeration.

I am sure his praise is well earned. How have you been doing Leonidas? Sleeping well?"

Leo chuckled, a bit uncomfortably.

"As well as I can hope to these days. And the days I struggle the clay medallions you gave me help significantly, so I have to thank you for those again."

Master Shepherd waved him off.

"It was no problem at all. Orpheus would have done the same for you if you had still been staying at the Academy, and I enjoy helping people when I can. I maintain my position here at Koyane Manor for precisely that reason. So if either of you need anything at all, please do not hesitate to come to me and ask. Even if I am not present, Tanya is very capable and always able to reach me in case of an emergency."

Leo nodded respectfully, though Isabella was certain he would never ask for help unless there was no other choice.

"Thank you. We will bear that in mind." Isabella said, trying to think of the most polite way to respond.

Master Shepherd smiled knowingly, then checked his watch when Tanya cleared her throat quietly.

"Well, I have an important phone call to make. I wish you two the best of luck in your investigation. I suspect you will be speaking with Allaran Dawnheart soon, so do please give him my regards."

Master Shepherd stood from his chair and turned towards the door.

"Tanya, please ensure they have everything they need before they leave."

Tanya bowed wordlessly and Master Shepherd quickly left the room.

"Would you like any refreshment before you go?" Tanya asked.

Leo shook his head, lifting himself out of his chair with a groan as if he had been sitting for hours.

"I'm good, thanks Tanya. Do you want anything Izzy?"

Isabella stood, more gracefully than Leo had, and shook her head.

"No, thank you. I still have some food left over from lunch, so I am set for a while."

Tanya bowed once again and motioned to the door.

"Then please allow me to escort you to your car, and if there is anything you need before you go, please ask."

"We follow your lead." Leo said dramatically, waving his arm in a wide sweeping motion.

Isabella struggled to resist the urge to slap him as they followed Tanya back out into the hall and headed back towards the foyer.

5

⠿

Chapter Five

"Could you answer a question for me?" Isabella asked, doing her best to speak clearly as the car rattled down a poorly maintained dirt road.

"I mean, I can try. Can't promise I have a good answer though." Leo said, turning his steering wheel back and forth slightly to try and miss the worst of the pot holes.

"Something has been bothering me about Koyane Manor. I am almost certain I have heard the name before, but I can't think of where. Looking back, it didn't even connect in my mind that it was an actual manor until we arrived there."

Leo nodded and tried to chuckle, though a particularly rough bump in the road just forced the air out as a grunt instead.

"That does make sense, believe it or not. I was the same the first time I went there with Detective Kardinal. I had already met with Master Shepherd once before, but he had actually stopped by my apartment so I hadn't had any actual reason to visit the Manor. I had remembered Headmaster Orpheus mentioning something about Koyane Manor, so that's probably where you heard the name too, most likely."

Leo paused for a moment, slowing down to crawl through a washed out section of road.

"Koyane Manor is kind of an open secret around Provo. Most people know it is over there, but most people choose to ignore it."

Isabella nodded, feeling her seatbelt lock and hoping that Leo would slow down a bit more.

"Why would people ignore such a beautiful estate and mansion?"

"Well, because most everyone who lives there is an Animal Aspect. And even though most people's Aspect has very little bearing on what they are capable of, some people still see them as basically wild animals that might go feral at any moment."

Isabella thought back to her interaction with Conner.

"That doesn't seem fair. Conner came across a little strange at first, but I was never really worried about him. And if miss Tanya is an Aspect, she was a paragon of civility and refinement. I didn't see any-one at the Manor that felt like they were not a normal person. Well, perhaps excepting Master Shepherd, but I think that was just because of how Headmaster Orpheus speaks about him."

Leo nodded, turning the car onto a slightly overgrown side road.

"To be fair, Master Shepherd is a bit different, considering he is probably one of only a couple people in the country who The Head-master would consider an equal."

Isabella blinked and felt her eyebrows rise in surprise. She glanced over at Leo, who simply nodded.

"Yeah, trust me, I felt the same way when I heard that."

Leo paused for a moment to go over another pothole before continuing.

"Master Koyane has multiple estates, in multiple different countries, and he has always taken in Aspects to work for him. He does it so that they have a place where they are accepted without concern for what they are. However, it is thanks to Master Shepherd that the estates are run with a high level of discipline and there is a focus on good manners. He is trying to change how people think of Aspects. People have heard too many stories about terrible things that happen around Aspects, so they think that is what a normal interaction with an Aspect is. Master

Shepherd is trying to focus more on standing out as polite, noble humans so that those bad stories will be eventually dismissed."

Leo pulled the car around a bend and onto a small gravel square that acted as a parking space in front of a narrow trail-head. He put the car in park and shut it off, placing his hands in his lap before speaking again.

"Though, they still have a lot of work to do. There are still a lot of people who treat Aspects poorly out of fear or prejudice. Then there is also..." Leo paused, debating on finishing his sentence.

Isabella could feel that the conversation had taken a heavy turn, and so she turned partially in her seat to face Leo, waiting for him to figure out what to say.

Leo took a long slow breath.

"There is a market for Aspects." He finished quietly.

The air in the car grew thick, and Isabella could feel Leo's power pounding in him like a drum. She carefully reached out and placed her hand on his. Leo looked down, taking a moment to recognize Isabella's hand, his power slowing back to normal.

"Sorry, It makes me a bit angry thinking about it. We do a lot of different things at Detective Kardinal's office, but we always drop almost everything if we get a case of an Aspect going missing. Even in a place as quiet as Utah, there is kidnapping and trafficking, but no one sells Aspects in the state for fear of Master Shepherd. If someone goes missing, we have to find them fast, or they get taken out of state to avoid the reach of Koyane Manor as much as possible. Master Shepherd hopes that, at some point, people will start to see Aspects more like the human beings that they are, and less like the power that has affected them. Then kidnappings will be far less common, and the ones that do happen will have more public support in finding them."

Leo sat for several moments, staring down at Isabella's hand, then shook himself.

"Thanks Izzy. Sorry for ranting at you." He turned his hand palm up and squeezed her hand slightly, then opened his door and got out with his usual grunting.

Isabella quickly got out of the car as well, meaning to say something else, but Leo started speaking again, facing the trail.

"Sorry to bother you like that. I was having a bit of a moment. We just wanted to speak with Master Dawnheart for a few minutes, if he is willing."

Isabella looked into the shadows caused by the thick tree cover over the trail, trying to see who Leo was talking to. Then, a slim figure in a thick, dark blue cloak moved out into the sun. The figure pulled their hood back, revealing an older woman with graying blonde hair and liquid blue eyes.

"You are lucky it was someone who would recognize you that was on guard today, Leo. Many of our younger members would have seen someone with such a fierce fire around them as a threat to the circle."

Leo chuckled and half bowed.

"I apologize for that, Lady Nightwick. I have had a lot going on and I wasn't truly focused on the task at hand. I hope we won't bother you for too long. This is my friend, and temporary partner, Isabella." Leo motioned over the car to Isabella. "She is much more well put together than I am, So I do hope you will let her come along."

Isabella nodded politely, and the older woman returned the gesture.

"Master Dawnheart said he was expecting someone to come and see him today, so he is already waiting for you in the cabin off the trail. He didn't want to bother you with walking all the way up to the main house."

"Oh, come on." Leo complained, scratching his head. "I'm not in that bad of shape, am I?"

The older woman harrumphed.

"You are young and resilient, much more suited to making the hike than Master Dawnheart. However, Master Dawnheart also claims that he wishes to maintain his youth through consistent exercise, and that your body is only half as strong as it once was. I think that is nonsense, of course, but I will defer to my leader's decision."

Isabella glanced at Leo's back, wondering what was meant by half as strong.

Leo laughed.

"Master Dawnheart is healthier than most men his age that I know of. Detective Kardinal always says he hopes to be in as good of shape when he gets to be the same age. I am sure if he didn't feel up to the hike, he would have let me walk up to the main house. I would personally never consider trying to tell him otherwise. Do we then have your permission to enter the forest, Lady Nightwick?"

Lady Nightwick sighed heavily and stepped aside, waving her open hand over the trail. Isabella felt a trickle of magic being used.

"You, Leonidas, and your partner, Isabella, have our permission to enter the Grove."

"Much appreciated." Leo said with a smile. He motioned to Isabella and she quickly followed him up the trail.

After a few moments of walking, after they turned a small bend, Leo glanced over his shoulder.

"Stay close and stick to the trail." He told her. "People tend to get lost if they don't have a member of the circle to guide them. The Grove doesn't care for strangers."

Isabella looked at the forest around them.

"Well that's comforting." She mumbled.

Leo answered with a short, unamused laugh.

"We have permission to be here, so the Grove won't try to swallow us outright, but we should stick only to where we need to go just the same."

They walked for several minutes before the trail opened up, following the edge of a small clearing. At the center of the clearing was a small, single room log cabin covered in moss.

Leo turned and made his way to the door, Isabella close behind. As they approached, Isabella could see symbols painted on the door and door frame depicting the sun, moon, and stars. Leo knocked and, after a mumbled reply from within, opened the door and stepped inside. He waited for Isabella to follow, then closed the door behind them.

The inside of the cabin was mostly bare, a simple wooden floor and a fireplace opposite the door being its only features. A window on either side of the cabin provided light for the room, and beneath one window a rocking chair had been placed.

It was with some amount of surprise that Isabella realized there was someone occupying the rocking chair. An old man with a long white beard wearing a long blue robe with silver trim sat quietly, looking out the window.

"It is such a clear and beautiful day today, isn't it?" The old man sounded almost wistful.

"It is." Leo replied. "Though I wish I had the time to actually enjoy it."

The old man nodded, starting to slowly rock in his chair.

"Indeed. It seems you have been caught up in something rather dire. Would that I were a few years younger that I may join your hunt."

Leo bowed slightly.

"I appreciate the sentiment, Master Dawnheart, but I am certain we will find what we need and your Circle needs you here. I wouldn't wish to take you from them."

The old man chuckled, finally turning his head to look at his two visitors.

"One of these years I will join the forest, and Katerine will lead the Circle. They have no real need of me any more."

"Oh, Come on Master Dawnheart, you've got plenty of time left. And loads of people still rely on you. I, for one, would be much less excited to come and consult with Lady Nightwick than I am to come speak with you."

The old man's eyes sparkled knowingly.

"Katerine comes across as gruff, but there are few more kindhearted than she. I am sure that, even after I am gone, She will be more than happy to advise you and Markov in your investigations."

Leo nodded.

"I certainly hope so."

The old man slowly stood up from his chair, then shuffled his way across the room and held out a hand to Isabella.

"Please forgive an old man for not standing immediately upon your entry milady. I am Allaran Dawnheart, I am pleased and honored to make your acquaintance."

Isabella accepted the old man's warm handshake.

"I am Isabella, it is a pleasure to meet you as well."

The old man nodded politely and then turned to Leo.

"You have brought such a lovely and polite young lady to meet me. Perhaps it is wise for you to ask the questions you need of me. Lest I chatter the day away."

Leo smiled politely, though he reached into his pocket and pulled out his notebook.

"Well, Izzy is much better at conversation than I am." Leo held the notebook out to the old man. "I was hoping you would look this over quickly for me. I don't think any part of it was specifically Wiccan, but I wanted to be sure. We don't really have a very clear picture yet, and anything we can rule out will be helpful."

The old man took a pair of spectacles out of a pocket in his robes and placed them on the tip of his nose, then accepted the notebook and opened it, skimming over Leo's notes.

"Hmm. An altar cover is common. Velvet is used on occasion, though many other things are acceptable and very few things require a specific cloth. Animal bones are traditionally used for prediction and future sight, but not in such a dramatic setting. A deer skull could be representative of a spirit or god, Though placed as it is reminds me more of Native American spiritualism than Wicca. Peach is a symbol of longevity, even Immortality. Plum is associated with pleasantness or young beauty. Cherry can be seen as good work."

The old man looked up from Leo's notes.

"A strange ritual indeed. It is no wonder you would find yourself seeking answers."

Leo nodded.

"Yeah. But even as weird as it looks, it still doesn't feel right. I can't shake the feeling of it being some sort of curse. There was power in everything but the circle of salt, flowing in spite of the police barriers. And it felt off when you walked in."

"Almost like you could smell something sickening, but when you tried to focus on it, it would go away." Isabella chimed in, trying to provide what little information she could.

The old man stroked his beard slowly a few times, handing the notebook back to Leo.

"Salt is tied to the earth, and is used primarily to mark boundaries between the physical and spiritual realms. It could have been used to protect the one performing the ritual from spirits. A bad feeling and smell that isn't there though, that is something I would expect to hear from individuals who are sensitive to magic. It is most likely natural energy, twisted out of its original form. What you might refer to as Outer Magic.

I believe your hearts know more than you realize, and I think you are correct in assuming it is a curse. However, curses do not come in only a variety that is used to harm others. Curses can also be used to try and pay a price to gain something. Much like summoning a spirit or demon to try and make a deal for power or wealth. I have seen individuals who sacrificed their health to try and gain more spiritual power. Or sacrificed one of their senses, sight being the most popular, to try and gain the ability to sense things outside of normal human perception, even the future."

Leo flipped open his notebook and scribbled a few notes down.

"Self cursing was not something I had considered." Leo said as he wrote. "That would explain the power leaving the police barriers, and the lack of an anchor point for the magic. I will have to follow that line of reasoning as well. Thank you, Master Dawnheart, you have been as enlightening as always."

The old man removed his spectacles and placed them back in his pocket.

"I am always happy to help, young Leonidas. It is people like they who performed that ritual that make others view magic in such a poor light. And if they are not caught, others will believe that kind of magic is an easy way to commit heinous acts without consequence. I believe that people like you and Markov will be the ones to help usher in an era of peaceful and prosperous magic. With the support of wonderful educators like young Master Orpheus and Master Shepherd, the world of magic will be able to breath a peaceful sigh of relief one day."

Leo half bowed.

"I hope I can live up to your expectations. And I almost forgot, Master Shepherd wished me to give you his regards."

The old man chuckled and shuffled back to his chair.

"He is quite the individual. Were that he had more time to visit with an old man like me."

"I am sure he would enjoy that as well, Master Dawnheart." Leo said, placing one hand on the door's handle. "But I think he takes on more responsibilities every day."

The old man nodded as he lowered himself into the rocking chair again.

"Well, then perhaps I will relax here and enjoy the view for a while for all of us. Until Katerine decides to come looking for me at the least."

"Then we will be on our way so you can have at least a few moments of peace."

Leo opened the door and motioned for Isabella to go. She half bowed to the old man and turned to the door.

"Goodbye Master Dawnheart. It was a pleasure to meet you."

"And you as well, young lady."

Isabella stepped outside and Leo made to follow her, pausing as the old man spoke from his chair with something akin to a warning.

"Take care of her, Leonidas."

Leo waited a few seconds before stepping through the door, answering quietly as he went.

"I could do nothing less."

* * *

Isabella looked around at the small apartment as Leo closed the door behind them. There was a side table between a simple rocking chair and couch in the small living room, and a small table with three wooden chairs around it in the connected kitchen.

"Make yourself at home." Leo said, hanging his coat up on a hook by the door. "It isn't much, but I haven't really had the time to decorate."

Isabella shook her head.

"No, it's about what I expected actually. Kind of reminds me of your room at the academy. At least you seem to keep it clean."

Leo chuckled, going into the kitchen and opening a cupboard to see what he had.

"You don't really have much confidence in me, do you? Not that I blame you. It's really only as clean as it is because I never have the time to get it dirty."

"Have you done anything to warrant confidence?" Isabella asked, sitting down at the table in the kitchen. "I know you have a tendency to forget to throw things away."

Leo furrowed his eyebrows.

"Hey, I throw lots of things away. I just don't want to throw away something I could use for something else. Are you opposed to having rice for dinner?"

"I'm fine with rice, as long as it isn't just rice. And you think you can use everything."

Leo pulled a box of minute rice out of the cupboard and set it on the counter. He grabbed a small sauce pan out of another cupboard and started filling it in the sink.

"Of course it will be more than just rice. What kind of peasant do you take me for?"

Isabella rolled her eyes.

"One that never eats vegetables. Your sandwich this afternoon was just meat and cheese. In fact, I don't think I have ever seen you cook anything more complicated than a bowl of cereal."

"Why does food need to be complicated?" Leo asked, setting his filled pot of water on the stove and turning it on. "I just don't see any need to add more than a few things. What's the point if you can't taste any of the individual things you are eating?"

Leo measured out some rice in a cup and dumped it in the water then he reached up in to his cupboard and pulled out a can of cream of chicken soup. He looked over his shoulder.

"Do you prefer corn or carrots?"

Isabella crossed her arms over her chest and leaned back in her chair.

"They are both good, but if I had to choose I guess I would pick corn."

Leo nodded and pulled a can of corn out of the cupboard. He opened a drawer and stirred around in it until he found a can opener and started opening the cans.

"Do you want me to help you with something?" Isabella asked after a few moments, but Leo shook his head.

"Nah, I've got it." He pulled a frying pan out and placed it on another burner on the stove. "I asked you to skip school and come help me out. Least I can do is cook you dinner. Besides, you have fed me food a bunch of times. I may not be a gourmet chef, but let me at least try to return the favor."

Isabella shrugged, trying to act like she didn't care one way or the other.

Leo opened his refrigerator, taking out a package of soft tortillas and a bag of pre-shredded cheese. He put a tortilla in the frying pan and then stirred the rice, deciding to drain off a little bit of excess water.

Isabella watched with something between interest and concern as Leo dumped the cream of chicken soup into the rice, followed quickly by the corn after he drained the water out of the can. He stirred the rice for a moment and then flipped over the tortilla in the frying pan.

Leo pulled out two plates from his cupboard and sat them on the table, then grabbed a small stack of assorted fast food napkins and put them in the middle of the table.

Turning back to the stove, Leo grabbed a handful of cheese from the bag and threw it in the rice. After a second of thought, he threw in another half a handful then stirred it all together until the cheese melted.

He pulled the tortilla shell out of the pan and placed it on a plate, then used his stirring spoon to scoop a few spoonfuls of rice onto the tortilla before rolling it tightly into a moderately sized rice burrito.

"For your dining pleasure milady." Leo said, turning to turn off the burner for the rice and to throw another tortilla shell into the frying pan.

Isabella scowled at Leo's back for a second, then looked down at her burrito, not quite sure what she was about to eat.

She picked up the burrito, careful not to let it unwrap, and selected a corner that seemed edible. Taking a bite, she could taste the savory soup and cheese with a slight hint of sweetness from the corn. She chewed a few times and swallowed, looking down at this strange new food.

"Well? How bad is it?" Leo asked, pulling a tortilla out of the pan and throwing in another one in almost the same motion.

"I'm not sure, but... I don't think I hate it."

Leo laughed as Isabella took another bite and chewed thoughtfully.

"Want something to wash it down? I've got tap water, I have milk, I have a couple sodas. I think I have some juice pouches somewhere."

Isabella swallowed her food.

"Juice pouches? Really? Are you five?"

Leo opened the fridge and stirred around before holding out a classic fruit punch juice pouch.

"They are pretty good." Leo said in a sing-song voice, shaking the pouch back and forth a few times.

Isabella scowled at him for a few moments before reaching out and snatching the pouch out of his hand.

"Fine, I'll take one." She said, pulling the straw off the pouch and stabbing it through the top.

Leo chuckled, pulling out a second pouch and sitting it on the counter for himself. He cooked for a little longer before turning everything off and moving the cooked food to the table and sitting down to eat his own dinner.

Isabella decided to eat a second burrito, then sat back in her chair and sipped at her juice pouch while Leo ate.

"Is this what you usually do every day?" Isabella asked, not really wanting to sit in complete silence.

Leo nodded and took a moment to swallow before answering.

"For the most part, though a lot of days I don't really have the time to get to cook and then sit down to eat. But, this case was big enough that Detective Kardinal wanted me to focus on it until we made some progress. About half the time I just pick up some fast food or a pizza or something on my way home because I am too tired to feel like cooking."

Isabella watched Leo for a few minutes as he ate, slowly realizing he was supporting most of his weight with his arms against the table and he had slight bags under his eyes. Several times she noticed an almost imperceptible flinch at the corner of his eyes as if he had been hit. She slowly sat her empty juice pouch down and leaned forward to get a better look, starting to remember how all the people they had met that day had interacted with him.

Leo's chewing slowed and he narrowed his eyes and turned his head too look at Isabella out of the corner of his eyes.

"What?" He looked down at the last bite of his burrito. "Are you eyeballing my burrito? I can make some more if you are still hungry."

Isabella shook her head slowly, her expression softer than usual.

"I'm fine, Leo. But I'm starting to wonder if you are."

Leo half smiled, throwing the last bite of his food in his mouth. He stood up from his chair with a grunt, which Isabella was beginning to realize he wasn't doing just to be dramatic.

"I'm fine, Izzy. In fact, the last few days have been really quiet so I am feeling pretty good. You don't need to be worried about me."

Leo grabbed the dishes off the table and sat them next to the sink, putting a plug in the bottom of the sink and turning the water on to fill it.

Isabella stood up and stepped over beside Leo.

"You cooked, so let me do the dishes. I would feel bad just sitting around and letting you do everything."

Leo chuckled, but stepped aside, knowing he wasn't going to win an argument with her.

Isabella expertly scrubbed the dishes clean, thinking over the day and organizing her thoughts. She started to put the pieces together and realized she was going to need to ask Leo some questions.

She dried the dishes off and stacked them neatly, draining the sink and toweling her own hands dry. When she turned around she found Leo sitting in his rocking chair with his head tilted back and his eyes closed, rocking slowly back and forth.

Isabella went into the small living room and sat down quietly on the edge of the couch, carefully inspecting Leo's face.

"You really don't need to worry about me." Leo said, without opening his eyes. "I promise I am fine."

Isabella frowned, not liking the fact that Leo read her so easily without looking.

"Can I ask you some questions? I want to understand some things."

Leo slowly stopped rocking in his chair. He took a few deep breaths then opened his eyes and looked directly into Isabella's. Instead of cracking a joke, like she expected him to, he simply nodded.

"Ask whatever you need to."

Isabella resisted the urge to nervously bite her lip.

"Lady Nightwick said you are half as strong as you used to be. What did she mean?"

Leo searched Isabella's eyes for a moment, and she could tell he wanted to look away. He took a deep breath and sighed heavily.

"Even though it's been over a year and a half, I still haven't fully recovered from the accident above The Academy. Physically, the damage has healed, but moving still feels stiff and achy, and I don't have the stamina I used to have."

Isabella felt a pang of guilt, and she could tell that Leo had noticed.

"You aren't at fault for that, Isabella. I merely took in more natural energy than you did so that I could tie the Leylines together. My injuries were a result of my own personal choice."

Isabella felt another pang. As much as she hated having her name shortened, she had also grown to not like hearing Leo say her full name.

"Then what are the medallions that Master Shepherd made for you? Why was he worried about how well you have been sleeping?"

Leo reached out and pulled open a small drawer from the side table, pulling out a small round disk of clay carved with runes and placed it on the table for her to see.

"When I drew in the natural energy of the Leylines I didn't have the time to properly mix that power with my own. My energy channels were severely burned. It took over a month before I could use magic again, and when I do it burns. The medallions suppress magic power to some extent. There was a long time where I couldn't sleep at all without one, because your power naturally ebbs and flows while you sleep. Now I can use most magic with little more than a slightly unpleasant tingle, but higher magic still burns and some nights I still occasionally need a medallion to suppress my power so I can sleep."

Isabella could feel her heart aching for Leo.

"And you still push yourself like this every day?"

Leo nodded.

"Only by living my life normally will I be able to heal back to the point I was before the accident. Headmaster Orpheus expects the healing process to take another two or three years. Taking it easy won't really take away the pain either. Besides, there are things going on in the world that are far more important than my personal comfort."

Isabella frowned, trying to think of some way to argue. Then she felt Leo take hold of her hand.

"Everything that can be done for me has been done." He said. "If I had to go back, I would gladly do what I did again. No matter the consequence, if I could have spared you from the pain and recovery you also had to go through, I would have. Worrying won't help either of us, so please..."

Leo stood from his chair, lifting Isabella's hand and lightly kissing the back of it.

"Just smile once in a while, and let me do what I can."

Isabella sat quietly, having gone slightly numb. Leo carefully placed her hand in her lap and then headed towards a small hallway.

"Let me clean up the bedroom and grab an extra blanket. You can sleep on my bed tonight. I'm more comfortable in the rocking chair anyway."

Leo disappeared into his room, leaving Isabella to stare at the back of her hand, trying to silently order her thoughts.

6

Chapter Six

Isabella blinked groggily as she heard a second knock on the door.

"Izzy? Sorry to wake you up, but Conner just called. They found a second ritual site. Police are sealing it off and they want us to come down and take a look at it."

Isabella yawned, remembering where she was.

"Ok, I'll be up in a minute."

"Take your time, we aren't in a huge hurry." Leo said, his voice trailing away as he went back out to the living room.

Isabella sat up with a yawn, trying to blink the sleep from her eyes. She stood up and stretched her arms above her head. She lifted her travel bag from the floor up onto the bed and opened it. After a few minutes of thought she decided to just wear a fresh set of clothes and shower after they got back from their investigations for the day.

After dressing and quickly brushing her hair, Isabella left the bedroom and made her way to the living room.

Leo was sitting at the kitchen table, looking at his phone and eating a bowl of cereal.

"Good morning." Leo said, typing something into his phone before setting it down and getting another spoonful of cereal.

"Good morning." Isabella replied, making her way to the table and sitting down.

"Sorry, all I've got for breakfast is cereal. I realize that I didn't plan very well for having a guest. I'll have to grab some groceries on the way back after work." Leo stood up and grabbed a bowl and spoon from a cupboard and sat it on the table in front of Isabella.

"That's ok, I don't mind cereal once in a while." Isabella responded quietly, picking up her spoon and poking at her bowl.

Leo chuckled and pulled a few boxes of cereal out of the cupboard and put them on the table for her to choose from.

"Still not a morning person I see."

Isabella scowled at him as he pulled a gallon of milk out of the fridge and placed it next to her before he went back to his own bowl.

"Mornings are fine, your bed is just uncomfortable and I didn't sleep well." Isabella grumbled, reaching for the first cereal box she saw that had marshmallows in it.

Leo nodded with a grin.

"Well I am sorry my pillow top mattress is not to your liking."

They finished breakfast in relative quiet. They quickly cleaned up and then grabbed their coats and headed out to the location Conner had messaged to Leo.

Isabella was still not fully awake and had to shake herself when Leo stopped the car in front of a large gym surrounded by police tape. Conner waved at them and Leo got out of the car, Isabella following a bit slowly behind.

"Glad you got here alright. Didn't get run off the road or anything?" Conner chuckled as Leo frowned.

"Fortunately not. I think it's early enough that we beat most of the stupid people out onto the road."

Conner half bowed to Isabella.

"Good morning to you, miss. Sorry for waking you up so early in the morning."

Isabella smiled and shook her head.

"Good morning. it's no bother, I usually have to wake up pretty early anyway."

"I'm glad it was not too much of a bother."

Conner turned back to Leo.

"Could you give me a quick ride back to the police station before you start? There are still some trails I want to follow, I just happened to find the site while I was looking into them."

Leo nodded.

"Sure thing, jump in. Do you want to come with, Izzy? Or wait here? Station is just a few blocks away from here, so it will only take a few minutes."

Isabella stared at Leo for a moment to process what he said, then she shrugged.

"I guess I can just stay here, no need to get in and out of the car a bunch of times."

Leo nodded and gave her a thumbs up.

"Cool. I will be back in, like, ten minutes or something. There is still an officer inside making his initial observations. You can go in and talk to him, or just wait out here if you don't like that idea."

"The site is in a small basketball court just inside the front door. You can't miss it." Conner added helpfully.

Isabella nodded, finally starting to fully wake up.

"Thanks. Guess I'll think about what I feel like doing."

Leo nodded and waved, turning back to the car with Conner following behind.

"Sounds good. Be back in a bit."

They got into the car and Leo started it up, turning it around and heading back out the way he had come in.

Isabella watched them go, then stood quietly by herself and looked around.

It was still early enough that the sun hadn't come out from behind the mountains yet, but she could see a few cars driving down the streets, and a handful of people jogging down the sidewalks.

After a few moments of watching, Isabella realized it might be a bit suspicious if someone saw her just awkwardly standing outside of a police marked crime scene, and she decided to go inside.

She pulled her detective badge out of her coat pocket and slipped through the police barrier, opening the front door of the gym and stepping inside.

She found herself in a hallway with several doors labeled as various workout and weightlifting rooms. A set of double doors on her left labeled 'Court' were propped open, so she walked over and peaked her head inside.

At the center of the basketball court was a makeshift altar with a few candles placed on it, surrounded by many symbols drawn on the ground with lines of salt in a large area. A plank of wood was propped up against the back of the altar with a deer skull and various trinkets hanging from it.

A figure with coppery black hair in a police uniform was standing several feet away from the altar, taking notes in a black, leather bound planner.

"Um, Hello. I came with Leo on behalf of Detective Kardinal to investigate the ritual here."

The figure froze, then slowly placed his pen in the planner and closed it.

"I... See. So he did bring you after all."

The moment the figure spoke, Isabella was hit with a horrific shock and unhappy memories welled up inside her.

The officer turned to face her, his brass name tag revealing what Isabella already knew, and it took every ounce of self control she had not to scream.

"Titus." Was all she could manage to say through her clenched teeth.

Titus slowly placed his hands at his side and then bowed deeply.

"I am afraid so."

Isabella clenched her fists then turned on her heels and faced the doors again.

"I will wait outside until Leo gets back."

"I understand." Titus said. "I... don't expect you to ever forgive what I did. But I do want to say, from the depths of my being, I am sorry."

Isabella paused mid step. A thousand angry retorts came to her mind, as did several violent spells, but something about his tone felt out of character for him. She chose not to turn around, not sure she could look at him without feeling more anger.

"How could I ever believe that?" Isabella struggled to keep her voice level.

"You don't have to. I wouldn't blame you for even a moment if you don't. The way I acted in the Academy was deplorable, and many people have every right to hate me. Not the least of which is you and Leo. I regret that it took such a horrible, life threatening, mistake for me to realize that I am not the great and powerful ruler I grew up believing I was."

Isabella chanced a look over one shoulder.

Titus stood at attention with an almost placid look of shame behind his eyes.

"While I laid in my bed, recovering, I swore to myself that for every moment I spent tormenting other people I would spend years serving them. As soon as I could move again, I joined the police academy. I can't ever undo what I did, but I can spend the rest of my life paying penance."

Isabella watched as he spoke, now torn in a whirlwind of emotions, unsure what to think of this unwarranted confession.

"I understand why The Academy forbids the sharing of our cards now." Titus said, more quietly. "The cards were never meant to tell others what we are. They are meant to tell us what we could one day be capable of. Had I realized, perhaps my mother's voice would not have swayed me."

Isabella thought back to the woman who had yelled at Temmy when she first woke up after the accident.

Titus looked down at the floor and an almost amused half smile crept onto his face.

"Though, had I known you and Leo's cards before the accident, I would have never dared pick a fight with him."

Now Isabella felt a wave of confusion, but before she could even begin to order her thoughts enough to ask any questions, Leo came around the corner.

"I hope things are going well here." Leo said, then leaned over and whispered only for Isabella. "Sorry."

"I've gathered most of the information I need here. So I can get out of your way if you need." Titus said with a nod.

Leo grinned.

"Oh, no worries Titus. It's a pretty open area, so you won't bother us any if you need to do anything else. Besides, someone insisted I bring them to see you."

Titus tilted his head with a strange expression, and Isabella gave Leo a confused look as he lifted his hand, holding out a magical silver tether.

"Can't I just come in now?" Came a forceful voice from behind Leo. Titus immediately frowned, his posture slumping as if in defeat.

"Why are you here, Charlie?"

Leo's grin broadened and he stepped further into the court. He was followed by a young girl with green eyes and long, coppery black hair. She was dressed in a gothic style dress covered in black lace, and carried a parasol made of a similar black lace. She kept her back perfectly straight as she walked, and Isabella thought she could easily have been mistaken for a life size porcelain doll.

Leo walked over to Titus and held out the tether, which Isabella could now see was extending from the girl's wrist.

Titus held out his hand, mumbling a few words, and the tether jumped from Leo to him.

"You know I'm working right now. Why are you here?" Titus repeated.

The girl pouted.

"The officers at the station wouldn't tell me where you were. Why shouldn't I be able to see my elder brother whenever I wish?"

Titus sighed and transferred his planner to the hand that held the tether and then pointed at the altar across from them with his, now open, hand.

"That is why, Charlie. I'm working right now. We have to take this altar apart in case there is a curse involved. It is not a place for a twelve year old girl to be running around."

The girl called Charlie looked over at the altar.

"Well, I mean, destroying it isn't that hard is it?"

She raised her parasol and a multi-colored flame ignited at the tip.

Isabella gasped, but before she could react Titus reached out and grabbed the tip of the parasol, extinguishing the fireball almost instantly.

"You can't just destroy it." Titus didn't quite shout, but his voice still echoed around the room.

Charlie pouted again.

"But why not?"

Leo chuckled, though he took a few steps to place himself between Charlie and the altar.

"Firstly, there is still evidence here that we need to find so we can catch whoever did it. Secondly, if it is a curse, and you just light it on fire, you could turn that curse back on yourself."

Charlie looked up at Leo with something akin to surprise.

"That can happen?"

"Yes." Titus said, clearly tired of the conversation already. "That is why Leo is here. He is going to investigate to see exactly what this ritual was for. Then, if it is a curse, he and his partner will break it the right way so it doesn't hurt anyone else."

Charlie looked Leo up and down.

"You can do that?"

Titus sighed heavily and Leo laughed.

"Yup. Isabella and I were trained specifically so we could break curses."

"I see." Charlie said, looking over at Isabella.

With a tug on her parasol to pull it out of Titus's grip, she walked back over and held her hand out to Isabella.

"I'm Charlie Angecles. Titus is my elder brother."

Isabella carefully took the young girl's hand.

"I'm Isabella. I am Leo's partner. It's nice to meet you."

Charlie nodded a few times, as if that was to be expected, and then flinched as Titus walked up behind her and knocked on her head.

"Be polite, Charlie. Father taught you better than that."

Charlie pouted at Titus, but shook Isabella's hand.

"Nice to meet you too." She said sulkily, glancing back at Titus.

"Can you actually break curses?" She asked, earning another knock on the top of her head from Titus.

Isabella smiled politely.

"Yes. As Leo said, we have been trained to break curses carefully so that no one gets hurt by them."

Charlie looked back and forth between Leo and Isabella a few times.

"Could I do that?"

Titus sighed again and Leo responded with a chuckle.

"If you want to study hard and learn to work well with others, I'm sure you could."

Charlie nodded once.

"I see. Then I will study so that Titus can have a reliable curse breaker he can work with."

Titus motioned towards Leo.

"I already know a reliable curse breaker. Besides, there is no way you would ever convince Mother to allow you to attend The Academy."

Charlie stuck her nose in the air.

"I wouldn't even bother asking Mother. I will ask Father, and by the time Mother is made aware of it, I will already be in training and it will be too late to do anything about it."

Titus grumbled, but Charlie pointed at Leo and spoke before he could complain.

"I am leaving you in charge of curse breaking. I expect you to support my brother in that capacity until I can relieve you of that duty myself."

Titus knocked on Charlie's head several more times and she tried to cover her head with her arms and parasol.

Leo chuckled again.

"Sure thing, Charlie. I'll help break any curses your brother needs broken. So no more need to go looking for him at crime scenes until you are trained and ready to take over for me."

Isabella could see Charlie's cheeks flush slightly pink under her arms.

"Well... good. Then I won't delay any longer in pursuing my training."

"Good." Titus said, taking hold of Charlie's shoulders and turning her towards the open doors. "Then you are going straight back home."

Titus glanced over his shoulder as he marched his sister across the basketball court.

"Sorry Leo, I will leave the rest to you. I have to make sure she gets back."

Leo waved with a big grin on his face.

"Bye Charlie. Make sure Titus goes back to work once you get home."

Isabella heard Titus grumbling as he turned the corner and disappeared from sight. She turned to see Leo pulling out his notebook and head towards the altar.

Isabella followed quietly behind, being careful not to disturb the trails of salt.

"Are you mad at me?" Leo asked, already scribbling notes in his notebook.

"Not... mad exactly. Did you know Titus was here?"

Leo nodded slowly, putting one hand on the side of the altar and then walking around the side to look at the deer skull.

"They always let me know what officers I will be working with."

Isabella frowned.

"And you still left me here with him?"

Leo spared Isabella a sad smile before turning to inspect the trails of salt.

"I called ahead to let him know you were with me, so he would be prepared to see you. I also know you would rather walk away from a conflict than lose yourself in a moment of anger. I had the utmost faith in you, Izzy. Besides," Leo crouched down and poked at some debris around the outside of the salt lines.

"I think Titus has truly changed, at least to some degree. I would have found it hard to believe myself not so long ago, so I knew you wouldn't believe it without seeing it for yourself. And I knew you wouldn't come inside to see him without me if I told you he was the officer on duty."

Isabella found herself feeling frustrated, almost desperate to feel angry.

"And you can forgive him for what he did?"

Leo paused for a moment, then stood up with a groan and walked over to Isabella. He put his pen and notebook back in his pocket then took both of Isabella's hands in his.

"If you mean the accident, I never blamed him for that. He didn't know what was at stake, and I didn't handle the situation well. I am just as much to blame, and he holds no ill will for it. So yes, for the accident, it never occurred to me not to forgive him."

Leo looked down with a frown for a moment, his thumb running across Isabella's fingers absently, his thoughts seemingly far away.

"If you mean how he treated you and Temmy... that will take me much longer to forgive."

They stood quietly for a moment and then Leo shook himself, seeming to remember where he was. He let go of Isabella's hands and took his notebook back out of his pocket.

"That said, I have watched him throw himself single-mindedly into every case I have worked with him on. If he continues to show that kind of dedication, especially to saving others like those he would have picked on in The Academy, then I think there is a world in which he earns some redemption."

Leo walked back to the altar.

"No altar cloth this time. Just a few simple candles. There is another deer skull behind the altar, but this time there are some charms hanging around it instead of tree branches."

Leo looked around at his feet.

"Lots of salt everywhere. Some fine bits of debris around." Leo paused for a second. "Is there any debris inside the trails of salt? Or is it just outside?"

Isabella blinked and remembered what they were supposed to be doing there. She looked down at her feet, but she was just surrounded by salt.

"I don't see anything over here."

Leo walked around to the outside of the ritual and crouched down again. He grabbed a pinch of the debris and placed it in one hand, spreading it around on his palm. He poked at it for a moment and then sniffed at it carefully.

"Coffee and bits of tobacco leaf. There is also some yellowish stuff here that might be corn meal. I will have to make sure that the police test it to make sure though."

"Coffee, tobacco, and corn?" Isabella moved over to Leo's side and he held his hand out for her to see.

"I am pretty sure. Coffee and tobacco both have pretty strong and distinct smells. The corn meal I am really only basing on the color and texture, so I could be wrong."

Isabella looked back around at the trails of salt. After a few moments she moved around to another side to look at it while facing the altar. She tried to stand on her tip toes to get a higher angle.

Leo noticed and followed her.

"What are you thinking?" He asked.

Isabella tried tipping her head back and forth.

"The salt isn't just laid out in a simple circle like the first ritual we looked at, and it doesn't look like runes or anything like that. What if it is supposed to represent something? Or outline something specific?"

Leo looked back at the salt trails.

"it's pretty big if that's the case. Probably fifteen or twenty feet long, if we don't include the altar."

Isabella nodded, trying to stretch higher again to try and see more.

"Do you want me to lift you up?"

Leo grinned as Isabella quickly took a step back and shook her head.

"Oh no, I don't want you to hurt yourself or anything."

Leo laughed.

"Come on Izzy, you're a toothpick. You weigh about as much as a wet blanket. I'm not going to hurt anything by having you on my shoulders."

Leo pulled his phone out of his pocket and held it out to her.

"Let me lift you up and you can take a few pictures so we can see if there is something we are missing from the ground."

Isabella slowly took the phone, still not sure she liked the idea. Leo crouched down and patted his shoulder.

Isabella frowned at him, but he just grinned back and patted his shoulder again. She sighed and carefully climbed onto his shoulders.

"Just don't strain yourself too much, ok?"

Leo responded by jumping straight up into a standing position, Isabella grabbing onto his head with a gasp.

"Leo!" She yelled.

Leo started laughing, making sure to face the altar.

"Take us some good pictures, Izzy. Try not to get the whole thing in one picture though, leave some parts out of each one."

Isabella scowled, but nodded and lifted the phone up and opened the camera.

She snapped a few pictures, trying to cut the edges of the ritual off on one side or the other on each picture. Then she held the phone down to Leo.

"There you go, you can let me down now."

Leo took the phone and slipped it into his pocket.

"Are you sure? Anything else you need to do while you are up there?"

Isabella grabbed the top of one of Leo's ears and tugged on it a few times.

"Yeah, I need to rip a certain someone's ear off for not putting me down."

Leo crouched back down with a grunt.

"You're no fun, Izzy."

Isabella climbed off of Leo's shoulders and then Leo sat down on the floor, pulling his phone back out of his pocket and opening it to look at the pictures.

"You're just going to sit on the floor?" Isabella asked, looking down at him.

"Well, I'm tired now." Leo said with a grin, flipping between a few pictures on his screen. He patted the floor next to him.

"Join me. it's pretty comfortable, all things considered."

Isabella sighed and sat down next to Leo and looked over his shoulder.

Leo looked back and forth at the pictures a few times, switching between them several times.

"Do you think...?" Leo trailed off, his head tilting to one side.

Isabella waited a few seconds for him to finish his sentence, and nudged him when he didn't.

"I usually think, yes. Do you?"

Leo nodded slowly, taking a few more seconds to answer.

"I do. And I think this might be a Veve. We might be dealing with Vodou."

7

Chapter Seven

"Yeah, there was still some active magic in the area. Isabella and I took it apart and then broke the salt lines to make sure it wouldn't reactivate. U-huh. Yup, should be clear to take it apart. There is some stuff around the salt lines that might be relevant though, so you should collect some samples and get them tested. If you do find anything else let me know. Yup. Thanks Titus. See you later."

Leo ended the call and started typing something on his phone.

"Will we need to do anything else for that site?" Isabella asked, putting a pot of water on the stove to boil while reading the instructions on the back of a box of pasta.

Leo sat his phone down on the table and stretched his arms above his head with a groan.

"Shouldn't need to. Not unless the police find something else while they are cleaning up the site. Our job now is to try and figure out the intention of the rituals and why they were left in such blatant public places. In town no less."

Isabella opened a couple of Leo's cupboards until she found a large bowl.

"I understand figuring out the purpose of the rituals, but does it really matter so much that they were in public places around town?"

Leo leaned forward and rested his elbows on the table, lacing his fingers together.

"In a smaller town, maybe not, but Provo is a different story. Most people trying to use magic like this usually try to hide it. Someone could be particularly brave, though, and just choose not to hide. However, Provo is a big city and it has several religious sites and temples. The faith of a lot of people flows through the city and drags natural energy along with it. There are several very large leylines that wind their way below the city that were attracted here by faith alone. Even the Lesser Dragon Line passes through here."

Isabella measured some flour into her bowl and added some salt.

"Faith can do that?"

Leo nodded.

"Faith is a powerful thing. And all those religious sites have their own... I wouldn't say power exactly. More like presence? A sort of weight of feeling when you are near them. The thing is that that presence, along with the flow of faith and the twisting leylines, has a tendency to mess with magic being used nearby. It makes it difficult to concentrate the energy needed to cast a spell, and it can make ritual magic exceptionally difficult to pull off. That's one of the reasons that the major factions that use magic, like Master Dawnheart's circle, live far outside the city limits."

Isabella looked over her shoulder while mixing some ingredients together.

"It didn't really feel too difficult to use magic to me."

Leo chuckled.

"Sorcery, in specific, is a little more resilient than most other magic. Of course, what we were doing was also relatively minor. Even sorcery starts to have problems though, once you start pushing into higher tiers of magic. Best I can compare it to would probably be people with strong Diamond cards. Their higher level magic gets disrupted because of some connection they have to something else that interferes, even though no one is quite sure what that something is."

Isabella nodded, turning down the temperature on her boiling water and dumping the pasta in.

"I guess that makes sense. I hadn't really thought about it that much before."

Leo leaned back in his chair.

"Really? You shared an apartment with Temmy for this long and you never thought about it?"

Isabella turned in surprise, nearly dropping the spoon she was using to stir the pasta.

Leo grinned, happily folding his arms over his chest.

"Let's be honest, Izzy. Anyone who has watched Temmy use magic before should be able to tell that one of her cards is a high level Diamond. If I had to guess, probably at least a Nine or Ten. She might even be an Ace."

Isabella blinked a few times, kind of stunned and not sure what to say.

Leo pouted.

"Oh come on. I've been in classes with Temmy just as much as you. I'm dense sometimes, but do you really think so little of me?"

Isabella opened her mouth to speak, thought better of it, and turned back to her cooking.

"Wow, so cruel." Leo whined.

Isabella laughed.

"You make it too easy." She said, pouring milk into her bowl to make a white sauce for the pasta. "But it's not really fair that you know what Temmy's cards are. Does she know yours?"

"Yes."

Isabella whirled around again.

"Wait, really? I was being sarcastic. Why does she know your cards? Why don't I know your cards?"

Leo grinned, trying not to laugh.

"Temmy is a genius. And she is more sensitive than she likes to let on. She honestly mostly figured it out on her own. I just kind of, failed to disagree with her assessment. Besides, if you pay attention, it isn't actually too hard to guess at least what kind of cards people have."

Isabella frowned and placed her hands on her hips.

"Well then what are my cards, mister expert?"

Leo leaned over in his chair.

"Is the pasta ready?"

Isabella pointed her spoon at him.

"Pasta is fine for another four minutes, don't dodge the question."

Leo slumped a bit in his chair.

"The Academy doesn't like us discussing our cards."

"We graduated, we can discuss whatever we want now."

"Can I plead the fifth?"

"Not if you want anything to eat for dinner."

Leo sighed dramatically, realizing he had talked himself into a corner.

"Alright, alright. Well, you have a large source of inner strength. You work well with others, and are an excellent multi-tasker. You always speak clearly and only rarely make mistakes, even when casting complex strings of spells. You are also very empathetic. You are good at understanding how other people feel, and seem to be skilled at learning healing magic from what I hear."

Leo tilted his head back and stared at the ceiling for a few moments.

"If I had to put forth a guess. You most likely have..."

Leo looked back at Isabella, then stood and walked over to her, leaning in and looking deeply into her eyes. After several seconds, and once Isabella could feel her cheeks starting to burn from how close he was, Leo stepped back.

"At least a high level Heart and a high level Club. One of them is likely an Ace."

Isabella blinked and felt her mouth fall open slightly. Leo sighed in relief and dramatically wiped his forehead.

"I am going to take that as meaning I was at least close." He said, walking back over to his chair.

"Did I waste enough time for the pasta to be done at least?"

Isabella slowly used her spoon lift a noodle out of the water and taste it, never taking her eyes off Leo.

"How...?" Her voice trailed off, trying to find words to express every thought going through her head.

Leo leaned against the table again, smiling, though he didn't appear particularly happy.

Isabella shook herself. She quickly dumped the excess water off the pasta and then added the mixture from her bowl. She stirred it around to coat everything, then placed it on the table and grabbed bowls and utensils.

She sat down and simply stared at Leo while he started to scoop pasta into his bowl. After a few spoonfuls he hesitated and sat his bowl down.

"Sorry, Izzy. I went a little overboard there. I could tell you my cards if it will make you feel better."

Isabella shook her head, suddenly realizing she was staring.

"No. It's alright. I'm the one who asked you to tell me what my cards were."

Leo tilted his head slightly to one side and gave her a knowing look.

Isabella sighed.

"I'm sorry, Leo. I really am. You are always making jokes, and teasing me, and being dramatic. I always forget that you are also really smart. I shouldn't. After final exams you were right at the top of the class with me and Temmy, but it never really occurs to me that you aren't dumb."

Isabella shook her head again and held up her hands.

"I'm sorry, that sounds mean. I don't mean that I think you're dumb."

Leo chuckled.

"I know, Izzy. I'll be honest with you, I don't like having to be serious. I go out of my way to keep things as light as possible, especially around you and Temmy. I like seeing both of you smile, and I want that to happen as much as possible. That's also why I asked Headmaster Orpheus to keep the extent of my injuries a secret. I knew you would worry, and I didn't want you to blame yourself or feel self conscious about how you treated me."

Leo lifted his bowl and started filling it again.

"I'll also admit I tried to keep myself extra busy so I wouldn't have time to come visit. That's why I didn't really want to bother you while you were studying to qualify to practice healing magic. I didn't really want to risk you figuring out I wasn't at one hundred percent."

Isabella frowned.

"So you did avoid talking to me for six months on purpose."

Leo grinned, placing his hands together as if praying.

"Please forgive me."

Isabella sighed and started filling her own bowl.

"Well, you did bring me a nice souvenir after the fact. I guess I will consider it."

Leo nodded.

"You are far too kind."

"I know." Isabella said, though she did smile.

"I was kind of right though. It only took you one day to figure it out." Leo said, grabbing his fork and spearing a few of his pasta noodles.

They ate mostly in silence, until Leo finished off the last of the pasta. With a groan, he stood and started gathering the dirty dishes to wash.

"What do you think you are doing?" Isabella asked before taking her last bite of food.

"Um, doing the dishes? I figured you cooked today, so I would clean up."

Isabella shook her head.

"Nope, that's my job."

Leo frowned.

"What kind of terrible host would I be if I made my guests cook and clean."

Leo's phone buzzed from his end of the table, and Isabella pointed at it as she stood up and took the dishes out of his hands.

"Nope, you have other work to do mister genius."

Leo blew a raspberry, then grunted as Isabella elbowed him. He walked back to the table and checked his phone.

"Oh, speaking of geniuses. My expert just messaged me that they have looked over the pictures I sent them of the ritual site from today."

"And what do they think about it?" Isabella asked over her shoulder as she stacked the dishes and started filling the sink with water.

Leo shrugged.

"I don't know. Let's call them and ask."

Leo pushed a few buttons on his phone then put it on speaker and placed it on the table. The phone rang several times and then beeped as someone on the other end of the line picked up.

"Um, hello?"

Isabella froze at the sound of the familiar voice.

"Leo? Why do I hear Temmy?"

Leo grinned.

"Oh, hello Isabella. How are you doing? Is everything going well?"

Isabella wiped her hands on a towel and turned to face the table with her hands on her hips.

"Hey, Temmy. I was doing fine until Leo told me he was calling an expert for help, but he never mentioned we were calling you. Not that I am upset that I get to talk to you."

"I... I wouldn't say I'm an expert."

"Sure you are, Temmy." Leo said, making sure to position himself with the table between him and Isabella. "I literally can't think of anyone anywhere near here with more expertise on the subject than you."

"Well, there isn't really a practicing Vodou community nearby, so that's not really saying much."

"Nonsense." Leo said, trying not to grin too much at Isabella. "I don't think there are many people as knowledgeable as you on most subjects."

"Thanks?" Temmy didn't sound convinced.

Isabella's eyes narrowed slightly and Leo cleared his throat.

"Well, Izzy will probably get mad at me if I don't ask what you think about the pictures I sent you."

Isabella harrumphed.

"You assume I'm not already mad at you." She muttered quietly so Temmy wouldn't hear.

"I think you were right in thinking that the ritual you saw was associated with Outer Magic, triggered by Vodou in specific." Temmy said, and they heard her typing on a keyboard.

"The pattern made from the salt makes a Veve that closely resembles the one representing Baron Samedi. It's not a perfect match, but based on the description of the rest of the site I think whoever did this was trying to contact him. Coffee, tobacco, and ground corn are all things that can be offered to him when his spirit visits. Though that is assuming that they managed to call on him. As I said, the Veve isn't perfect. Most likely it was made by someone unfamiliar with any true Vodou traditions, so there is no guarantee that a spirit was called at all. And if there was one, it could have ended up being anything. I doubt they actually called on the true Baron Samedi."

Leo nodded, listening carefully to everything Temmy said.

"So you think that whoever did this was someone who doesn't really know about the magic they are using?"

"I think that whoever put together the ritual understands the basics of how magic functions, but it seems like they are just getting bits and pieces of things and using them without actually learning how those pieces are meant to be used. Unless there is something that unifies all the parts that we aren't seeing, I would guess that this person was never officially trained to use magic."

A beep sounded on the phone. Leo picked it up and looked at it.

"Hey, sorry Temmy. I need to hang up on you. I'm getting a call from one of the police officers on the case.

"Ok, I will let you know if I find anything else."

"Thanks, Temmy. You're the best."

"Bye Temmy." Isabella called out and then Leo ended the call and put the phone up to his ear.

"This is Leo."

Leo listened for a few seconds and then his features hardened.

"Got it. We'll be there in a few minutes."

Leo turned off the phone and rushed over to the door to grab his coat.

"Leave the dishes Izzy. Titus says Conner just called for backup. He's cornered a suspect several blocks south of us in an apartment complex."

Isabella quickly shut off the water for the sink and grabbed her coat, putting it on as Leo opened the door for her. Leo closed the door behind them and they both rushed to get to his car.

* * *

"Stay with Conner. He will make sure the guy doesn't get away if he runs, so I need you to back him up."

Leo held out a handful of small yellow beads, and dumped them into Isabella's hand.

"Charge these with magic and fling them if you or Conner gets attacked. A few seconds after charging them they will burst and stun anyone they make contact with."

Isabella nodded, transferring the beads from one hand to the other.

"What about you?"

Leo shrugged off his coat and threw it over the hood of his car.

"I'm going to go around the other side of the apartments so we can make sure that nothing happens until the police get here. Titus was already coordinating with the rest of the department when he called, so it shouldn't be long before they get here. Then they can go in and catch the guy. We are just here in case of curses or magical discharge, and as back up if all else fails."

Leo rolled back his sleeves to his elbows.

"You'll also keep an eye on Izzy, right Conner?"

Conner nodded, holding his mask open so he could smell the open air clearly.

"I'll bark if we run into a problem."

Leo half smiled.

"Izzy, if he starts barking, slap that muzzle of his shut."

Isabella nodded, trying not to smile.

"I'll see how it goes."

Leo nodded back before heading around the side of the building that faced the main road. He found no entrances and continued around to the back.

The street in the back of the apartment building was much smaller than the main road, but it still had parallel parking along the shoulder.

Leo spotted a door and walked over to investigate it. It was a simple white door with the words 'Employees Only' printed in simple black lettering. A tug at the handle told Leo the door was locked and he decided to check the other side of the building before picking a place to keep watch from.

Leo made his way towards the narrow alley that led between the apartment building and the buildings next to it. As he turned the corner, he paused.

A man, with bleached blonde hair and tattoos on his neck and one arm, who was wearing a black tank top and baggy black pants, was climbing his way down the fire escape.

Leo took a couple quiet steps forward and then leaned nonchalantly against a dumpster in the end of the alleyway, watching the man climb down as far as he could before dropping down to the ground with a grunt.

The man looked over his shoulder towards the front of the building as he stood and started walking towards the back.

"Nice day for a walk." Leo said.

The man jumped, his head whipping around to face Leo.

Leo grinned.

"Jumpy fellow aren't you. Something going on I should be worried about?"

"Do yourself a favor, kid, and mind your own business."

The man sounded like he had been gargling rocks.

Leo nodded and pushed himself away from the dumpster.

"You're probably right. My business today is finding someone who performed a couple pretty dramatic rituals this past week. Don't suppose you know anything about that?"

The man scowled and raised one hand.

"Dirty Pig." He growled, conjuring a dirty orange flame in his hand that looked like it was made by burning plastic.

"That's not very nice, I showered recently. Besides, pigs are great. You must at least like bacon."

A bolt of fire shot past Leo's head, slamming into the building across the street and leaving a scorch mark on the brick.

Leo continued to grin, his sharp gaze challenging the man in front of him.

"Your power is unstable. I wonder what you might have done to cause that."

The man conjured more fire, using both hands now, and shot two more bolts at Leo.

Leo raised his right hand and batted both projectiles out of the air with one swipe.

"Can't we just talk about it? I don't think there is any need for this."

The man lowered his stance, held his arms out to his sides, and shadowy smoke began boiling off his shoulders and back.

Leo's grin faded to an annoyed scowl.

"You really shouldn't play with things you don't understand."

The man looked up at him, his eyes glazing over until they turned black. He raised up and stepped forward, slamming his hands together to release a wave of darkness towards Leo.

Leo felt his body burn as his power rose. A red aura of power surrounded him and he placed his hands together, thrusting them forward and splitting the wave of darkness around him. As the darkness passed, he stepped forward and waved his arms in a wide circular motion behind him. The darkness shuddered and responded to him, coiling around him and gathering in his hands. He pulled the darkness into a single orb between his hands then fired it back at the man, striking him in the chest and knocking him off of his feet.

The man hit the ground and rolled several times before standing up with a grimace, one hand placed gingerly over his chest. He gave Leo an angry look before turning to run the opposite way.

Leo watched him go several steps before a dark haired figure stepped out at the other end of the alley. He felt a small surge of power and the man fell back, covered in a web of arcing electricity.

Titus stepped further into the alleyway and put another yellow pellet between his thumb and forefinger. Another surge of power caused the pellet to glow, and Titus flipped it with incredible speed into the man. Another surge of electricity caused the man to collapse to the ground.

"Glad you got here when you did, Titus." Leo said, walking down the alley and meeting Titus over the, now unconscious, man.

"Why didn't you stun him yourself?" Titus asked, crouching down and pulling out a set of handcuffs.

Leo chuckled and scratched the back of his head.

"He attacked me without letting me try to talk him down. Plus I kind of gave all my shock pellets to Isabella before I came around here."

Titus glanced up at Leo as he pulled the man's arms behind him and cuffed them together.

"Yeah, I guess that sounds about like what I would have expected."

Leo shrugged.

"It let me guess at what the guy had been doing at any rate. His power is unstable. Not quite flickering, but waxing and waning in uneven beats. And it seems almost muddied, thicker than it should be."

Titus rolled the man onto his back and pulled an iron medallion out of a pouch on his belt. He held it up at eye level and recited some words. Runes engraved on the metal blazed to life and he placed it on the man's chest.

"Sounds like someone who is mixing magics."

Leo nodded.

"Also possible he is using more than one source of Outer Magic. On that note, should check to ensure he isn't possessed or haunted by a spirit too. His eyes lost all light while we fought."

Titus stood and pulled the radio off his chest.

"Good call. Thanks for your help, Leo, I'll take care of the rest."

Leo nodded and started making his way back to the front of the hotel as Titus radioed in that the suspect had been apprehended. He waved to a few officers as they rushed around the corner to back up

Titus and headed back towards his car. Isabella and Conner were waiting for him.

"Is everything ok?" Isabella asked. "I felt something awful."

"And I smelled it. Had to close my mask that guy's smell was so bad."
Conner's forehead scrunched as he spoke through his mask.

Leo chuckled and picked up his coat off the hood of his car.

"Yeah. Guy was aggressive right from the start. But despite having
something going on, he definitely was never trained to use magic. He
tried running, but Titus cut him off and got him. They used a medallion
to seal his power, so it's just a matter of the police taking him in to
custody now."

"So what do we do now?" Isabella asked.

Leo stretched and groaned for a moment and then fished his keys
out of his pocket.

"Well, I was planning on going home and soaking in a hot shower
before going to bed. Unless you had something else you wanted to do."

Isabella smiled.

"A shower and bed sounds like a great plan."

8

Chapter Eight

Isabella lay on her back, staring up at the ceiling of Leo's bedroom. Her mind swam in unending spirals, thinking over everything they had done in the last couple days.

After glancing at the clock for the fifth time, and finding it was only a minute later than the last time she checked, she sighed and sat up, throwing the blanket off of her. She quietly opened the bedroom door and slipped out into the hallway.

Leo was sitting in the rocking chair, eyes closed, slowly rocking back and forth.

Isabella could see a faintly glowing clay medallion sitting carefully on his chest. She walked quietly down the hall into the kitchen and pulled a glass out of the cupboard. She filled it with water out of the sink and took a slow drink.

She watched Leo's hair peeking over the top of his chair for a few minutes, sipping at her water.

"Are you awake?" Isabella eventually whispered.

"Maybe." Leo mumbled back. "Couldn't sleep?"

Isabella placed her glass next to the sink with a sigh. She walked around Leo's chair and carefully sat down on the couch near him.

"Had a lot going on in my head. Was keeping me awake, so I decided to get some water."

Leo nodded, his eyes still closed, continuing to slowly rock in his chair.

"Anything in particular on your mind?" He asked.

Isabella thought quietly for several moments.

"I'm not sure." She said, a note of frustration in her voice as she slowly laid back against the couch.

"I keep thinking over everything we investigated. Everything fits what we reported. The guy Titus arrested admitted to casting rituals at both sites to gain magical abilities. And yet, every time I think through it, I find myself starting from the beginning again. I feel like I've missed something, but there isn't anything that doesn't make sense."

Leo's eyes cracked open slightly, watching Isabella as she spoke.

"Do you think we caught the right guy?"

Isabella nodded.

"Yeah, he definitely felt like he had been mixed up in something. And Conner said the guy was definitely the one he had smelled at both sites. There isn't any reason I wouldn't believe we got the right person."

Leo carefully lifted the medallion off of his chest, the runes engraved on it slowly ceasing to glow, and placed it on the side table. He leaned forward and rested his elbows on his knees.

"Do you think there might be more than what we saw on our first inspection?"

Leo waited patiently as Isabella opened and closed her mouth several times, trying to think of words to say that would match what she felt.

"I don't know." Isabella sounded upset. "There isn't anything we saw, or that was reported, that didn't fit in to everything the guy confessed to."

Isabella leaned forward, putting her face in her hands.

"I don't understand why it's bothering me."

"Can I ask you a question, Izzy?"

Isabella looked up, straight into Leo's eyes. A look she had never really seen from him before filled her with a strange sensation of both calm and tension.

"Yeah?"

"We talked about cards at dinner, and I told you what I thought two of yours were. Is your last one a Diamond?"

Isabella slowly nodded.

"Y-yes. A Two of Diamonds." A thought popped into her head. "It was my first draw."

"Base of Power." Leo mumbled, opening the drawer on the end table and pulling out his phone.

Leo typed a few numbers into his phone and held it up to his ear. After several seconds someone on the other side answered.

"Hey, this is Leo from Detective Kardinal's office. I know the Provo Ritual case is officially closed, but I wanted to ask if it would be possible to put a hold on the clean up of the two sites."

Isabella blinked, surprised that Leo would go to that length.

"Yeah, I understand. Thank you. Let Officer Angecles know I will swing by first thing in the morning and he can finish the clean up once I am done. Yup. Appreciate it. Bye."

Leo ended the call and sat his phone down.

"The first site is already cleaned up, but they haven't opened the warehouse yet so we can still go snoop around one more time. The second site was cleared of salt and debris, but everything else is still intact."

Isabella just sat and quietly looked at Leo.

Leo looked around behind him and then back at Isabella.

"What?"

Isabella shrugged.

"I don't know. I'm not sure I expected you to take my late night insecurity seriously."

Leo laughed quietly, leaning back in his chair and rocking again.

"I probably don't go out of my way enough to inspire confidence for you either. Even if we have caught on to everything going on at the site though, I would rather spend the time to go back over it than miss something important."

Leo smiled at Isabella.

"Besides, I may be sarcastic and joke with you all the time, but I will always take you seriously. You feel like something is wrong, I will do whatever I can to help you figure out what it is."

Isabella sat quietly for a moment, not entirely sure what to think about what Leo had said. After another moment of sitting quietly, and not wanting to sit in silence, She finally asked another question that came to mind.

"What made you think my last card was a Diamond?"

Leo continued to rock back and forth slowly.

"People who have Diamonds are known to have keen insight. Most psychics and soothsayers have at least one Diamond card. And every Seer who ever received clear visions of future events were always high level Diamonds. I asked because, if you did have a Diamond card, most likely there was something that was trying to tell you we missed something. Especially since you also have a high level Club, as they are known for their empathy. And the Diamond being your first draw makes it doubly likely."

Isabella thought back over everything she had been taught about the ceremony for drawing cards.

"The first draw is the Base of Power. The source of strength and inner power."

Leo nodded.

"Diamonds, as the Base of Power, opens the mind to the world. Allowing clear sight of all things."

Isabella thought about what the meaning of her other cards would be, then shook herself slightly.

"What... What was your first draw?"

Leo's rocking slowed to a stop.

Isabella held out one hand.

"You don't have to answer that if you don't want to. It was a stupid question."

Instead of answering her, Leo reached out and took hold of her hand. After a few moments he waved his other hand, and released a trickle of magic. A click sounded at the end of the dark hallway, and a small, ornately carved, wooden box slowly floated down the hall and settled into Leo's open hand.

"I… now know all of your cards." He said, carefully placing the box in his lap and opening it to reveal three cards face down on a silk cushion. "it's only fair that I show you mine."

Isabella started growing tense.

"What are my cards? Tell me first. I want to know specifically, Leo."

Leo looked up at the ceiling for a moment, and Isabella realized he was nervous.

"Your first draw, Two of Diamonds. Your second draw, Ace of Clubs. Your third draw,"

Leo's breath shuddered slightly and he turned his head to look at Isabella.

"Queen of Hearts."

Isabella felt herself squeeze Leo's hand tightly, a warm flame lighting in her chest.

"Yes." Was all she could force herself to say.

Leo looked down at the three cards in the box on his lap. He carefully reached out with his open hand and rested it on the first card.

"My first draw."

He flipped the card over.

"Ace of Hearts."

His hand moved over to the second card.

"My second draw."

He flipped the card.

"Ten of Spades."

His hand moved over, hesitating over the third.

"My third draw."

Leo paused, his hand frozen in place.

Isabella could feel her heart beat rising and the warm flame in her chest grew hotter. Her open hand reached out, as if of its own volition, and pushed Leo's hand down to the bottom of the card. Then she took hold of the top and nodded, the pounding in her chest telling her what she was about to see.

Leo carefully nodded back and they turned the card over.

"King of Hearts."

Leo's voice faltered, and he wasn't able to look Isabella in the eye.

Isabella felt her cheeks flush. She carefully lifted the box off of Leo's lap and placed it on the side table. She stood, took hold of Leo's other hand, and gently pulled him to his feet. She waited a few moments and then asked a question.

"Even when you tease me, you are always kind. Why do you treat me so well?"

Leo bowed his head, staring at the floor, his eyes a cloud of emotions. He stood silently, for several moments, before he was able to answer.

"Every time I see your face, my heart races. It tells me to make you happy, that your smile is the most important thing in the world. My heart wants to stay at your side, and I cannot deny it."

Isabella felt tears welling up in her eyes, her heart trying to beat out of her chest.

"Why have you never told me?"

Isabella could feel Leo's hands trembling.

"I was... afraid that if I said anything, you would push me away. I didn't want you to treat me differently, and I didn't want to lose our friendship altogether. My...My heart couldn't bear the thought."

Isabella smiled, wanting to laugh and cry at the same time. She let go of Leo's hands and carefully wrapped her arms around his chest and hugged him tightly, resting her head on his shoulder.

"You are a fool, Leonidas."

She felt his arms gently rest on her back, returning her hug.

"I am a fool. And you, Isabella, are the Queen I serve."

* * *

Isabella leaned against one wall of the basketball court, yawning.

"Tired?"

Isabella shook herself and looked over, watching Titus walk into the room while pulling a pair of blue latex gloves over his hands.

Isabella nodded.

"Yeah, I didn't get much sleep. Too much going on in my head."

Titus nodded in return.

"Dispatch told me Leo needed to check through the sites today before we finished clean up. I understand the feeling of missing something makes it hard to sleep. I've had a few sleepless nights over it myself."

Isabella nodded, looking over at Leo, who was wearing a pair of latex gloves identical to Titus.

"I'm not sure how Leo isn't tired though. I kind of bothered him in the middle of the night about it."

Titus chuckled, which Isabella found to be strangely not unpleasant.

"I think he is always tired. He seems to function the same no matter when I see him or how much he has been doing. it's like he is a car that always has the low fuel light on, but he never seems to run out of gas."

Titus pulled a few evidence bags out of his pocket.

"Then again, I am a Spade through and through. My power is sharp, but relatively limited."

Isabella looked over at Titus.

"Oh, was that..." She trailed off, thinking better of her questions.

Titus gave her a knowing look.

"Yeah. I am the King of Spades. We don't have to keep it a secret anymore. I drew two spades and a club. I am built for combat but, other than the King, my other cards are pretty average. I am pretty much exactly the opposite of Leo. Hearts have a lot larger reservoir of strength to draw from, it's just slower than Spades."

Isabella nodded a few times and then did a double take to look at Titus again.

"Wait, you mentioned that before. How do you know what mine and Leo's cards are?"

Titus tapped on his name badge.

"Police keep a record of what is drawn by everyone who goes through the drawing ceremony. Makes it easier to narrow down suspects when you can see which people are capable of specific types of magic. We kind of use it like a magical fingerprint."

"That... makes a lot of sense actually."

Before Isabella could say anything else Leo made a sort of victory noise.

"Hey, Titus, lend me a hand."

Titus quickly made his way over to Leo, who had pulled all the charms off the board at the back of the altar and pulled the board itself away.

Leo pointed to a paper tag stuck to the back of the altar where the board had been before.

"There is a Taoist paper tag here that I didn't see before."

Titus crouched down beside the altar to get a closer look while Leo carefully laid the board down on the floor.

"Looks like one used for trapping spirits." Titus said as Leo joined him.

"Think you could deactivate it without burning it?" Leo asked. "If I stop the flow of power in the tag it will likely burst into flames."

"They do tend to do that." Titus said, handing two of his evidence bags to Leo.

"But I might be able to separate the tag into pieces and seal them before the magic turns back on itself."

Leo nodded and took a step back as Titus pulled his latex gloves off.

Titus placed his hands together in front of his chest, palms together horizontally with one hand pointing left, and the other right. He took a few slow breaths, then one deep breath before speaking a string of spells.

Isabella felt a sudden burst of power and pushed herself away from the wall, now fully awake.

Titus gathered power and concentrated it in his hands. A deep blue aura of power settled around him as he deliberately slid his hands apart until only the tips of his fingers were touching, keeping them near his body. The power gathered in his left hand took on a deep, nearly black, color. The power in his right turned a bright sky blue.

He slowly tucked his pinky and ring fingers in under his thumbs, compressing the power into his pointer and middle fingers until it hardened like a blade. Then, twisting slightly to the right and sliding his left foot forward, he pulled his hands apart in a shower of sparks.

Titus lunged forward, swinging his left hand in a slashing motion across the back of the altar. He quickly twisted, swiping his right hand across the same path. A loud cracking sound echoed around the room, and a blue flash of light wrapped itself around the altar before fading away.

Titus spun on one foot, maintaining his balance as he twisted and placed his hands together in front of his chest again. A few more words and the power gathered around his hands disappeared and the aura of power around him faded.

Leo quickly dropped to one knee, holding his hand out to the tag. After a few seconds he grinned.

"Nice job, Titus. Complete cessation of magic flow. No magic is going to cascade from this now."

Titus nodded, taking a small case from his belt and pulling a pair of tweezers out.

"Good. Glad it worked out. Been a while since I tried casting two spells at once."

"And yet here you are, doing it like an old pro."

Leo held one of the evidence bags open as Titus carefully peeled the top half of the paper tag off of the altar, revealing a clean, diagonal cut around the half way point.

Titus placed it in the bag and Leo sealed it, then held out the second bag and did the same for the bottom half of the tag.

Leo held the two bags up side by side and carefully inspected them.

"Izzy, I think this might be what we were missing before." Leo said, holding the bags out for her to see.

Isabella walked over and took them, looking over them herself.

"This looks a lot different than the other stuff here." She said, handing the bags over to Titus to see.

"It definitely feels different than the rest of the ritual site. The ritual was kind of just put together, but this tag feels very purposefully crafted." Leo scratched his cheek while he spoke.

He looked over at Titus.

"Did you find anything like this at the first site?"

Titus shook his head.

"No, but the concrete block that was being used for the altar was pushed up against a support beam for the warehouse, and we didn't take that when we left. Judging by this one though, there could very easily be a tag on the back of that altar as well. Trapped between the altar and the support."

Leo nodded.

"I will let you take care of that. I'll borrow one of those tag pieces you have there and I will swing by and talk to Conner. See if anyone besides our main guy messed with the tag. Then we should probably go sit down and have a chat with our main suspect."

Titus held out one of the evidence bags.

"Just make sure to check it in to evidence once you get back. I'll take a few people over to the first site and check for tags there. I don't know if they will let us interrogate the man we arrested until they have gone through the process of sealing his power completely, so it may take a couple days before we can do that."

Leo took the evidence bag with a shrug.

"Well, hopefully, there shouldn't be anything active going on here now. So we shouldn't need to be in a hurry to talk to him. I don't think I like the direction things are going though. This seems like an awful lot of effort for just a guy who wants to be able to use magic."

Titus nodded his agreement and turned, heading towards the door.

"Well, what do you think Izzy?" Leo asked, looking down at the charms laid out on the altar.

Isabella looked around the room.

"I'm not sure. You said it seemed like a lot of effort for someone to use magic, and I agree. It seems to me like there are much easier ways to be able to do that. Ways that don't involve the risks of Outer Magic. And why does he want to use magic so badly he felt the need to perform multiple complicated rituals? There has to be a reason, right? He wouldn't do it just to do it would he?"

Leo chuckled.

"Maybe we will turn you into a detective yet. Those are excellent questions."

Isabella felt her cheeks burn and turned away, sticking her nose in the air. Leo chuckled again, carefully folding the evidence bag and putting it in his pocket.

"But, lets not get too far ahead of ourselves. Lets go pay Conner one more visit."

Isabella nodded.

"That sounds like a place to start at least. And I wouldn't mind saying hello to Miss Tanya again."

Leo grinned and rubbed his stomach as he walked towards the door.

"Maybe she will offer refreshments again. Breakfast was kind of small."

Isabella hit Leo in the shoulder as he walked past her.

"You were the one who only wanted a bowl of cereal because you were in a hurry. Next time eat something more filling."

Leo pouted at Isabella as she followed him out.

"But cooking takes so looooong." He whined, dragging out the sentence and then running as Isabella lifted her hand to hit him again.

9

Chapter Nine

Isabella watched Leo open the door to the police station and walk back to the car. He opened the car door and slid inside with a grunt.

"What did they say?" Isabella asked.

Leo pulled his seat belt over his shoulder and plugged it in, then stuck the key in the ignition.

"They said we can have an interview with the guy they arrested in a few days. But they said they closed the case completely, since the guy admitted to casting the rituals and summoning spirits for personal gain. So if we want to investigate anything further we have to do it on our own time."

Leo turned the key and started the car, shifted the car into gear and looked over his shoulder to start backing out of his parking spot.

"That doesn't really seem fair, since we found new evidence."

Leo nodded, signaling and pulling out onto the road.

"The police are more concerned with the fact that he did it, and less concerned about why. Plus they have to pay Detective Kardinal for every day we spend investigating."

Isabella frowned, crossing her arms over her chest.

"Well what did Detective Kardinal say?"

Leo shrugged, slowing down to let someone change lanes in front of him.

"Detective Kardinal agreed that the job they hired us for is essentially over, since we were just supposed to find out who did it. But he did agree to give me another week of personal time to keep investigating if I want. So unless something bad happens that he needs me for, I can do whatever we think we need to."

Isabella looked over at Leo, watching him for several minutes as they drove. As they pulled into the parking lot of Leo's apartment building, she finally spoke.

"I'm sorry Leo. If I hadn't said anything you wouldn't have to worry about any of this."

Leo blew a raspberry as he shut the car off and they got out.

"You don't need to be sorry about anything. I'm glad you told me you were worried about the case. We found something we might have missed otherwise. Like I told you before, I would rather waste some time going over everything again than potentially miss something important."

Isabella followed Leo up the stairs, still feeling a little guilty.

"Thanks, Leo."

Leo chuckled and they kept going until they got to Leo's apartment. He checked the mail box next to the door, pulling out a couple of letters, then unlocked the door and held it open for Isabella before following her inside and closing the door behind him.

Isabella hung up her coat next to the door, Leo doing the same while looking through the letters he had brought in.

Leo paused on a blank envelope, flipping it over to look at the back.

"Weird. Someone put a letter in my mailbox without any address or anything."

Isabella went into the kitchen, opening Leo's cupboards to try and decide what to have for lunch.

"Maybe it's a letter from the apartment owner?"

Leo shook his head, sitting down and setting the other letters on the table.

"I don't think so. He has my phone number if he needs to get a hold of me. And the apartment building sends announcements via email."

Leo tore open the envelope and pulled out a handwritten message.

Isabella froze as she felt a sudden rise in power. She looked over to see Leo scowling angrily, a faint red aura settled around his shoulders. She carefully stepped over to the table.

"Leo?"

Leo's eyes scanned over the note several times before holding it out to Isabella and pulling out his phone.

Isabella took the note and read over it.

"Detective. Stop looking into matters that do not concern you. Something terrible might happen to that pretty young lady you have been bringing home if you don't."

Isabella felt like she had been punched in the gut.

Leo held his phone up to his ear.

"Hello, Tanya? I am sorry, I know I just left there, But I need you to have Conner drop whatever else he is doing and come to my apartment. We just received a letter to stop investigating the ritual case. Yeah, I understand that. The problem is the letter is threatening Isabella and I am not willing to put her at risk by leaving the apartment again right now. Thanks, I'm sorry to ask you for this right now, but I really appreciate it. I'll try to make it up to you and Master Shepherd later."

Leo hung up the call and started dialing again.

"Izzy, do me a favor and close the bolt lock on the front door."

Isabella nodded and put the letter down on the table, and then walked over to the door as Leo lifted his phone to his ear again. She slid the bolt on the front door shut, and felt a small surge of power flow through the door and walls as she did.

"Hey, this is Leo from Detective Kardinal's office. I need to speak with Officer Angecles please. Thank you."

Leo paused for several seconds, and Isabella could see his foot tapping nervously on the floor.

"Hey, Titus. Sorry to call you right after leaving. We received a threat at my apartment to stop investigating the ritual case. Yeah, I already called Conner and he should be heading here shortly. No, we will be fine here. The apartment itself is protected, and anything strong enough to get in is something you are going to feel all the way across town if it tries. I'll make sure that the only people who touch the note are me and Isabella. Thanks Titus. Appreciate it."

Leo hung up the phone and put it down, knitting his fingers together and resting his hands on the table.

Isabella could see Leo was clasping his hands together so tightly his knuckles were turning white. She quietly moved back over to the table and sat down beside him, carefully placing a hand on his.

Leo took several long, slow breaths, his power slowly calming down and his hands relaxing.

"I'm sorry, Izzy. I shouldn't react that way. Titus is going to come and see if the apartments have cameras and ask around to see if anyone saw someone leaving the note. And he will meet Conner here and then call me to let me know so I can let them in."

Isabella shook her head, and squeezed Leo's hands.

"It's ok. I appreciate you looking out for me."

Leo took another deep breath and sighed loudly.

"I'm still sorry. I should have better control of my temper. But someone choosing to threaten you is just..."

Leo let his head hang and closed his eyes, unable to speak without getting angry again.

Isabella tried to position herself in front of Leo as much as she could and took hold of his hands with both of hers.

"It's ok. I've gotten angry wanting to protect people I care about more times than I can count. You are allowed to be angry. Not one person would blame you for being angry."

Isabella tried too look at Leo's face, eventually reaching out and lifting his face gently so he would look at her.

"It's ok to be angry." She repeated.

Leo half smiled, turning his hands up and squeezing Isabella's hand.

"Thank you, Izzy. I don't deserve it, but thank you."

Isabella sighed, lifting one of Leo's hands and resting her cheek against it.

"You don't get to decide whether you deserve it or not. I've decided you do. Only thing you get to decide is if you want to keep investigating or not."

Leo's eyes sharpened for a moment, but quickly softened again.

"Of course I am going to keep investigating. There is someone out there doing something they don't want anyone to know about, and they threatened to hurt you. As long as they are out there, they could decide to try and come after you. Even if we decided not to investigate, the chance they choose to turn on you anyway is too high. I don't want to let you get hurt, and I don't want to worry about what I might do if you did."

Isabella smiled, still nuzzled against Leo's hand.

"You are a good person, I know you will do the right thing no matter the situation."

Leo chuckled softly.

"I will strive to live up to your opinion of me."

Isabella laughed, giving his hand one more squeeze before standing up.

"Don't worry, my opinion of you is pretty low, so I'm sure you can reach the goal."

Leo pouted, though his lips were trying to smile.

"So cruel."

* * *

Leo waved to Conner and Titus and then shut the door, sliding the bolt shut. He took a moment to take a deep breath and then made his way over to his rocking chair and gingerly lowered himself into it.

"So we are planning to wait here until we can interview the guy we caught yesterday?" Isabella asked, stacking some dishes from their dinner next to the sink.

Leo nodded, slowly rocking in his chair and considering whether or not to get one of his clay medallions.

"Yeah, Titus will make sure the police route their patrols past us to keep an eye out, and Conner will see if he can find anything based on the smell of the note."

Leo heard his phone ring and fished it out of his pocket. He paused for a moment when he saw the name. He answered and slowly put the phone to his ear.

"Hello? Oh, hey Headmaster."

Isabella glanced over her shoulder, quickly wiping her hands off and moving to sit down on the couch by Leo.

"Yeah, we are fine. I have my apartment sealed, and the police are patrolling around the area, so we should be pretty safe here. Yeah, she's here with me."

Leo glanced at Isabella and nodded a few times.

"Yeah, I can do that, gimme a sec."

Leo took his phone away from his ear and put it on speaker, holding it out closer to Isabella.

"Hello?" Isabella leaned in to speak closer to the phone.

"How are you doing Isabella?"

The Headmaster's voice was conversational, but Isabella could tell there was also an amount of tension she rarely heard from him.

"I'm doing pretty good. Would be better if Leo had a healthier variety of food, but I'm making it work."

The Headmaster chuckled.

"I don't doubt it. Leo has always been a picky eater."

"Hey." Leo complained. "I like plenty of things. I just don't always make a lot of food at home, so I wasn't prepared to have someone here who wanted to cook."

"Will you have enough food if you decide to stay inside your apartment for the next few days?"

Leo nodded.

"Yeah, we did some shopping yesterday. And I have enough canned stuff to feed us for weeks. Plus, Titus offered to bring us supplies if we needed them."

"Oh. Were you alright, Isabella? Meeting Titus again I mean."

Isabella sighed heavily.

"I can't say I was very happy about it. But... he honestly looks and acts so differently from the way he did at the Academy that I found myself almost forgetting who he was before."

"That's good." The Headmaster sounded relieved. "His Father asked me to recommend him to the police academy a few months after the accident. It appears that spending months in bed gave him the time to think over his actions. He seemed sincere enough, so I sent the recommendation. I'm glad to hear that that recommendation was not wasted."

"Titus appears to be a model officer." Leo said. "The first time I worked with him it took me a couple looks to even realize who he was. And then he decided to throw me off by bowing and apologizing for a bunch of stuff. Honestly, if he keeps going the way he is, I think he could do really well for himself."

Isabella found herself nodding along with Leo's statement, and wasn't sure whether she was happy or not to be agreeing with him.

"That's good."

The Headmaster paused for several seconds.

"Are you doing alright, Leo? You're sounding a bit worn out."

Leo chuckled, scratching the back of his head.

"I'm good. I just kinda stressed over that note we got more than I should have."

"Did you end up... over exerting yourself?"

Leo chuckled again, though not as sincerely.

"You don't need to dance around it anymore. I broke down and told Izzy about the problems I have been having. Well, she kind of mostly figured it out herself. Yeah, I might have over done it a bit. But I have a bunch of medallions on hand that Master Shepherd made for me, so I should be fine."

"I see." The Headmaster sounded like he was not at all surprised.

"If that is the case. Isabella? Would you do something for me?"

Isabella shuffled forward on the couch.

"Of course. Anything."

"Before you left, you were learning how to tune yourself to another person to help promote healing. Could you do that for Leo? It won't truly heal any damage, but it will help to alleviate some of the pain.

"She doesn't really need to..."

"I can do that." Isabella interrupted Leo, giving him a scowl to keep him quiet.

"Excellent. It should be good practice for you while you are away as well. And Leo? Try not to work yourself up too much, you know it won't do you any favors."

Leo sighed.

"Yeah, I know. I try not to, but this was a bit of a special case. Not that that is really an excuse."

The Headmaster chuckled again.

"I understand. I would like nothing more than to come and protect the two of you myself. Unfortunately I have far too many responsibilities at The Academy, and I am painfully aware that the two of you are capable of taking care of yourselves nowadays."

Isabella smiled.

"Leo and I can take care of things here. I hate to say it out loud, but I think Leo and I together can handle almost anything."

There was silence on the line for several moments before the Headmaster spoke again.

"Leo?"

Leo took a few seconds, nodding his head at the question behind the question. He looked over at Isabella and then answered.

"Yeah, I... kind of spilled the beans. Went overboard explaining how to guess someones cards and guessed what hers were. I ended up showing her mine in return."

Isabella felt her cheeks burn and was glad the Headmaster could not see her through the phone.

"I see." The Headmaster sounded like he was smiling. "Then I will say, as the King and Queen of Hearts, the two of you have an enormous amount of synergy together. Not just for working together either. I have never really had the two of you cast magic together, at least not by yourselves. That was by design. As you both know, Royal suits are often drawn together by their fates. The King and Queen of Hearts can cast magic far and beyond what either of you could cast alone. The synergy exists for all Royal Suits of course, but Hearts in particular are the best at it. I guess this is a long winded way of saying, if anything at all happens, stand together and you will be fine."

Leo scratched his head again, and Isabella could see a touch of color on his cheeks. She smiled at him and spoke.

"Don't worry, Headmaster. You trained us well. We will be alright."

"Yeah, we've got this handled here." Leo said, trying to stare at the phone so he wouldn't have to make eye contact with Isabella.

"Glad to hear it. But, if you do run into any trouble, please call me. Or at least Master Shepherd, if it is an emergency. And don't feel bad about it either. There is nothing either of us is doing that requires us so much that we cannot come to you if you need us. And both of us have more support in our work than we like to rely on, so nothing bad will happen from us leaving our posts for a while."

Leo shook his head.

"Nah, we will be fine. The only thing I think we need to be worried about is Izzy getting bored and throwing me out in the next couple of days."

Isabella glared at Leo and the Headmaster laughed on the other end of the line.

"I'm sure Isabella won't find that necessary."

"I don't know." Isabella said. "Leo does seem to specialize in being aggravating."

"I'm sure the two of you can work it out." The Headmaster said with another chuckle. "I'll talk to the two of you again another time. Be safe."

"We will." Isabella said. "And if you see Temmy, tell her I said hello."

"I will. Goodbye you two."

Both of them said goodbye and Leo ended the call with a dramatic sigh.

"I almost had a heart attack when I saw it was Headmaster Orpheus calling. I was trying not to tell him anything so he wouldn't worry, but

I guess Master Shepherd probably caught wind of what was going on and told him."

Isabella nodded, and stood up from the couch.

"Yeah, that makes a lot of sense. I would tell you off for not letting the Headmaster know, but I would have done exactly the same thing."

Leo chuckled, and then paused as Isabella held her hand out to him. "What?"

Isabella gestured with her hand.

"The Headmaster asked me to do something, and I might as well do it now."

Leo looked at her hand for a moment and then remembered what she was talking about.

"Oh yeah. You really don't need to bother yourself."

Isabella reached down and grabbed Leo's hand, tugging on his arm.

"Come on, up you go. Lay down on the couch. I'm not going to let you tell me no, so don't bother."

Leo sighed, sticking his phone in his pocket, and stood up with a dramatic groan.

Isabella gave him an annoyed look and kept holding on to his hand until he sat down in the middle of the couch.

After a few moments of her staring daggers at him, Leo finally gave in and turned, laying back and resting his head on the armrest of the couch.

Isabella pushed his legs up onto the couch and then knelt down on the floor near his head. She took his right hand in her left, and then rested her right hand over his heart.

"I haven't really done this before, so stay still until I figure it out. Try to keep your power flowing evenly."

Leo nodded.

"I am at your mercy doctor."

Isabella scowled at him, but closed her eyes and concentrated.

Several minutes went by in silence, and Leo found himself trying to breathe in slow, even breaths. Then, all at once, he was flooded by a wave of warmth that chased many of his aches away.

Isabella let out a long sigh and opened her eyes, which were wet with unshed tears.

"Do you always feel like this?"

Leo nodded slowly.

"Today I'm more sore because I built up too much power worrying, but it's still not really much worse than normal. I really don't want you to worry about it."

Isabella frowned, tipping her head to one side and resting it against Leo's hand.

"Of course I am going to worry about it. If you always push yourself, and always hide how awful you feel, you're going to suffer needlessly. I don't want that."

Leo looked over at Isabella and just watched her for a few moments.

"Every day I push myself, I hurt. But each day after that it hurts just a little bit less. Every day things get better and, eventually, the pain will go away. I promise I am fine. Please, don't worry. There is no need for both of us to suffer."

Isabella sighed again, closing her eyes and pressing Leo's hand against her cheek.

"Don't suffer alone, Leo. Let me be here for you. Let me take some of that pain away."

Leo carefully laid his free hand on the one Isabella had on his chest.

"I am pretty sure I told you that the best thing you can do for me is smile once in a while. Seeing you happy always brightens my mood, and I forget about the pain for a little while. That's honestly all I need."

Isabella lifted her head and opened her eyes. Leo smiled at her.

"I know that sometimes I make it difficult, so I will try to not be as much of a nuisance."

Isabella half smiled, though her lip trembled slightly.

"You also told me you didn't really want me to treat you differently. The same goes for me. It would be weird if you started acting really differently. Besides, we both know you can't help yourself. First chance you get you're going to say something sarcastic."

Leo's smile widened.

"That doesn't sound like something I would do."

Isabella smiled back, resisting the urge to hit him. She sighed and rested her cheek on his hand again.

"At least let me do something like this for you once in a while. I don't want to feel like I can't do anything for you."

Leo nodded once.

"Well, the Headmaster did tell you to practice."

Isabella nodded back.

"Yes he did."

Leo sighed loudly, but he smiled and brushed her cheek with one of his fingers.

"I will always try to talk you out of it, but I just can't tell you no. Besides, I'm not dumb enough to think you would accept no for an answer anyway."

Isabella laughed.

"I'm glad we understand each other."

They sat in companionable silence for a while, no more words passing between them. Eventually Isabella let go of Leo's hand and carefully stood up.

"What should we do after I finish with the dishes?" She asked quietly, walking into the kitchen.

Leo shrugged, closing his eyes and folding his arms over his chest.

"Doesn't really matter to me. I have some cards and board games we could play. I haven't turned the TV on in a while, but I am sure that it probably still works."

"Hmm." Isabella tried to make it sound like she was thinking hard about it as she put the dishes in the sink and turned the faucet on.

"Temmy taught me a new card game a while ago. We could play that."

Leo nodded, yawning and shifting his position on the couch slightly.

"That sounds fantastic. Temmy always comes up with great card games."

Isabella nodded, grabbing the first dish and a sponge.

"She does, doesn't she."

Chapter Ten

Leo took the folder Titus handed him while Isabella looked out through the one-way glass at the man in the other room.

"I never really got a good look at him before. He seems kind of... off."

Titus nodded.

"The receptionist told me the same thing while she was booking him originally. Couldn't tell me why, just that he was uncomfortable to look at. I thought that was a bit strange coming from someone who deals with criminals every day."

Leo flipped through some things in the folder.

"He unnaturally manipulated his magical channels. Even if you don't have the knowledge and ability to check that directly, the human mind is phenomenal at detecting things that aren't the way they should be. Probably why it didn't bother you that much, Titus. You already knew what was wrong with the guy without really having to think about it."

"Perhaps." Titus said, moving to stand near the one-way glass.

"Anything specific you want me to ask him?" Leo asked, closing the folder and heading towards the door.

Titus shook his head.

"He has already given us everything I need from him. You're pretty good at interrogations, ask whatever you think you need."

Leo saluted and stepped out into the hallway, walking down to the door to the interrogation room and letting himself in.

"Hello, good sir. How are you doing this morning?"

The man frowned.

Leo sat down, setting the folder in front of him.

"Oh come now, I know we got off on the wrong foot the other day. I really did just want to have a chat."

The man stared off into the corner somewhere above Leo's head.

"I already said everything I had to say."

Leo nodded, opening the folder and putting his finger on the first page.

"Sure thing, um, Stanton. Can I call you Stan?"

The man continued staring silently.

Leo nodded some more.

"Stan it is. Listen, Stan, I know what you told the police. And they are perfectly happy with what you gave them. I, however, am not the police, and I have a few things I would like to clear up."

"What does it matter?" The man never chose to look at Leo.

Leo shrugged.

"Lets call it academic curiosity. I just want to understand everything I come across. And the first thing I want to understand is, why go through the effort? To try and gain power, I mean. There are classes available for people who want to learn magic. Even if you aren't adept at sorcery, there are other options."

"I wouldn't expect someone like you to understand." The man continued to stare off into space, but his frown started to turn into a scowl.

"Hmm? Oh, you mean my magic. I know it seems easy for me, but I have trained for well over a decade to reach that level. I can assure you, I was no expert when I started."

The man's eyes glanced at Leo for a second, then returned to their place above his head.

Leo nodded again.

"Lets move on to the second question." Leo said lifting a few pages out of the way and pulling out the evidence bags containing the pieces of the Taoist paper tags.

"What were these tags for? There was one on the back of each of the altars you set up. The rest of the rituals seemed pretty complete, so I am a bit stumped as to what these are for."

The man looked down, but as soon as he saw the tags his eyes snapped back to the corner of the room.

"Just what the ritual called for."

Leo nodded, lifting one of the bags and looking at the tag inside.

"So you were following a set of instructions then. Where did you find them?"

"Someone gave 'em to me."

Leo pulled a pen out of his pocket and scribbled a few notes on one of the papers in the folder.

"I see. Was it the same person who gave you the paper tags?"

"I made those along with the ritual."

Leo chuckled.

"Oh come on Stan, you and I both know that's not true. Takes more years of training than I have had to make perfect paper tags like these. Definitely more training than someone who is performing rituals to gain powers has."

The man scowled.

"Yeah, whatever, same person."

Leo nodded again, this time with a grin.

"I see. And what, exactly, did they get out of this? Were they just helping you out of the kindness of their heart?"

The man grumbled, pressing his lips tightly together.

"I will take that as a no. Did you pay them for their services? Or did they ask you to do something for them in return?"

The man shook his head, keeping his lips pressed together, but he spared another glance at the table.

Leo nodded, jotting down a few more notes.

"So using the tags themselves was the favor you were asked to do."

The man flinched, looking at Leo with unpleasant surprise.

Leo didn't look up from his note taking.

"I know I don't look like it, Stan, but I am a detective by trade. Figuring things out is kind of my thing."

The man frowned deeply.

Leo sat his pen down, resting his elbows on the table and lacing his fingers together.

"Look, I am going to be honest with you, Stan. Your prison time is basically set in stone. So nothing else you can say here, short of admitting to a bunch of other crimes, is going to change anything one way or the other. So hiding things from me won't help you. Now, I know there is someone out there who helped you set this up. And whether you knew it or not, they had an ulterior motive for doing so. In fact, whatever they are doing seems important enough to them to send out threatening letters to try and get people to stop looking into it."

The man looked down at his own hands, refusing to look at Leo again.

"Whatever they are doing, it is drastic enough that they are afraid of people finding out what it is. When we do find out, and I assure you we will, if anything they did is attached to the rituals you performed I can guarantee they will try to use you as a fall guy for it. I am sure neither of us want that."

The man continued to stare at his hands, slowly opening and closing them.

"Well, Stan? What do you say? Help me out. Don't let someone blame you for their own wrong doing."

The man sat quietly, obviously going through some sort of internal struggle. Eventually he shook his head and grumbled.

"Alright, man. I don't know exactly what they were doin. They were tryin to make some fancy thing, but they said they had to get some sort of seed or something first and..."

The man paused, his mouth moving wordlessly, and Leo jumped to his feet.

"Isabella! I need you! Now!!"

The man lurched forward, coughing up blood. Leo rushed around the table.

"Titus! He needs an ambulance!"

Leo tried to put his hand on the man's back, but he got pushed away.

The man coughed up more blood, shakily grasping at the folder and grabbing Leo's pen. He started quickly drawing something as Isabella rushed through the door.

She ran over and tried to sit the man upright, but he shrugged her off, trying to push the folder towards Leo.

"She is a healer, let her help you." Leo said.

The man tapped on the folder urgently, starting to go limp.

"I got it, I'll take care of it. Let us help you."

Leo pulled the folder away from the man, and Isabella finally got him to lay back in the chair. She placed one hand on his chest and the other on his forehead.

"He losing a lot of blood internally Leo."

Leo nodded, placing his hands on either side of the man's face.

"He had a curse placed on him. I don't know if it was triggered by what he said, or if someone activated it from a distance. Do what you can to try and keep him alive while I try and break the curse."

Isabella nodded, closing her eyes to concentrate, a bright red aura settling around her as her power rose.

Leo glanced over his shoulder as several officers rushed into the room.

"If there are any other healers or cursebreakers here we could use their help. Keep everyone else away until the ambulance gets here."

One officer turned and began giving orders, and another, younger officer rushed over to Leo.

"I'm a cursebreaker, I don't have much experience, but I will help any way I can."

Leo nodded, turning back to face the man.

"Just lend me whatever strength you have, I will take care of the rest."

Leo felt the officer place his hands on his back, and power flowed into him. With a deep breath Leo started speaking a long string of spells, opening his mind and searching for the source of the curse.

A few moments later, another surge of power flowed into Leo, this one more familiar. Leo pulled from this new source of power and reached deeper into the mind of the man before him.

After several more minutes of searching, Leo found a single anchor planted deep in the man's mind. Attached to that anchor was a black thread filled with an almost rancid feeling power.

Leo changed his tone and spoke a new litany of spells, charging the anchor until it, and the black thread, burned away under the tide of power.

Leo finished his spell, closing himself off to the officers helping him.

"I got it." He said, looking over his shoulder at the officer from before.

"Good." Titus said, lifting his hand off the younger officer's shoulder.

Leo turned back to Isabella.

An older woman with completely white hair had her hands on Isabella's shoulders, sharing her power.

"I don't know if I can save him." Isabella said, sounding strained. "The damage is really severe already."

Leo reached out and placed his hands on each of Isabella's.

"Then take my strength too."

A surge of power burst through the room as Leo and Isabella's auras merged into a brightly burning red flame that enveloped them and the man.

Titus and the other officer fell back, covering their eyes. The older woman merely lowered her head and continued to provide what power she could.

Several minutes passed under this new tide of power, and only when the EMT's arrived with the gurney did the aura fade.

Isabella let her hand's fall to her sides tiredly.

"His lungs are in bad shape. I was able to keep them from collapsing, but they need attention right away. He also has a lot of intracranial pressure that needs to be relieved. The rest of his body is probably damaged as well, but those are the most pressing issues."

The EMT nodded once.

"We will take it from here."

"I broke the curse that started the cascade, but I would have a cursebreaker at the hospital on standby just in case." Leo said, leaning against the table.

The EMT nodded again, and they all watched as the man was lifted onto the gurney and rushed from the room.

After they left, Leo hung his head and sighed heavily, teetering slightly. He felt someone put their arms under his to steady him.

"I'm ok, Thanks Izzy."

He looked up at her and smiled, noticing how pale her face was. He wrapped one arm around her and pulled her closer, supporting both of them against the table.

"And don't pretend you aren't just as tired as I am."

"I'm too tired to argue with you at least." Isabella said, resting her head on Leo's shoulder.

"I'm glad you two were here." Titus said, putting on a pair of latex gloves. "If you weren't, he would have been gone long before anyone could have gotten here to save him."

Leo nodded slowly as Titus looked over his shoulder at the other officer.

"Go get the supplies from the cleaning station, and have Officer Polland open a new file for an investigation into an attempted homicide by curse."

The officer saluted and rushed from the room.

"I think I will take my leave." The older woman said with a bow.

"Thank you for your help, I would have struggled a lot more without you." Isabella said, never lifting her head off Leo's shoulder.

"I was happy to help. You did well dear."

With another bow, the woman left the room, leaving them in relative silence.

"Feel free to take as long as you need." Titus said quietly, picking up the, now blood-stained, folder from the table.

"Thanks Titus. And thanks for lending me some power to break that curse."

Titus nodded, checking the contents of the folder.

"Of course. I wasn't about to stand by and let a curse take someone in my own office."

Leo looked over his shoulder at Titus.

"It was activated at a distance by the way. It was anchored pretty deep in his mind, deeper than a subconscious trigger would reach. So whoever did it must have realized he might give them up and tried to finish him off."

"Strange that they wouldn't have attempted this immediately after his arrest. There wasn't anyone else here besides us who would have heard what he was saying, so how did they know he would say any-thing?" Titus flipped the folder over as he spoke and frowned. "Though, perhaps he did give them up."

Titus held out the folder and pointed at the image the man had drawn.

"What do you make of that?"

Leo looked at the image for several seconds, the wheels in his tired brain turning slowly. It was just a crude sketch of a cylinder, surrounded by multiple circles, with what looked like a stick figure at the center. Then a light seemed to turn on and his eyes widened.

"That... shouldn't be possible."

Titus looked between the image and Leo a few times, and Isabella tried to lift her head off Leo's shoulder to look.

"Are they trying to build a Reliquary?"

Titus's eyes also widened. He rushed over to the door, trying not to get blood from the folder on anything.

"I need a camera and fresh evidence bags in here."

Titus turned back to Leo.

"I think your case might have just gotten reopened."

* * *

Leo flipped slowly through an old, leather bound tome, skimming over the pages. Isabella lounged on the couch with her head near the side table with a stack of books and notes.

"Have you found anything yet?" Isabella asked, setting one book aside and picking up another.

Leo shook his head.

"Not yet. I'm kind of doubtful I'm going to have anything here that talks about Necromancy in any sort of detail. I think I will end up having to call The Academy and see if we can get permission to go through the older restricted tomes they have in the library collection."

Isabella nodded, setting her book in her lap and stretching.

"Yeah, I wish I had gone to more effort to study it while I was there. I'm supposed to train to counter the negative effects of those kinds of magic for my healer certification, but I put it off since that's still a ways off for me."

Leo yawned, closing his book and placing it on the side table.

"That's ok Izzy, I doubt you would have come across anything about making a Reliquary anyway. It's one of those forbidden magics that's just really hard to be able to study. A lot of paperwork has to get filled out, and you almost feel like the knowledge corrupts you as much as actually using the magic would, it's a pain."

Leo stood up from his chair with a groan.

"I don't even think there is anywhere in Provo that even has the necessary licenses to have any books on the subject at all. Our only options, short of flying across the country to a repository, are The Academy and Koyane Manor. Headmaster Orpheus is authorized to hold on to pretty much any text on magic. And Koyane Manor has a sizable collection of older tomes that Master Shepherd might let us comb through if we need to. Though there would be no guarantee that any of those would have what we need either."

Leo headed towards the kitchen and Isabella propped herself up on her elbows.

"I can cook some dinner if you are getting hungry." She offered.

Leo shook his head, smiling at her over his shoulder.

"Take it easy for tonight, Izzy. You aren't used to exhausting yourself like you did today."

Isabella pouted as Leo opened the fridge and stared at it's contents. After a minute he shook his head and closed the door.

"I think I might just order a pizza. I don't really feel like making anything myself either."

Isabella laid back and picked up her book again.

"You know what? Tonight I will let you get away with that."

Leo grinned and took out his phone. After a quick call to the pizza place, he walked back over to his chair and plopped himself down in it with a grunt. He spent a few minutes typing on his phone and sent a few messages. Once he got a reply he dialed a number and placed the phone to his ear.

"Hello Temmy! How are you this fine day?"

Isabella quickly put her book down.

"No fair, I want to talk to Temmy too."

"Glad to hear it. Hold on just a second, Izzy wants to say hello."

Leo sat his phone on the side table and set it to speaker phone.

"Hello Temmy. How have you been doing?"

"Hello Isabella. Everything is fine here. It's been pretty quiet."

Isabella sighed, leaning back so her head was closer to the end table.

"That sounds nice, It got pretty hectic around here today."

"Really? What happened?"

Leo quietly made an X with his arms and shook his head, and Isabella nodded.

"Just a lot of work to do. We are both pretty tired."

"Speaking of work," Leo said, rocking in his chair. "Are you busy right now Temmy?"

"No, I just finished working on my project this morning and I was thinking of waiting until the weekend to pick up another one. Why? Do you need something?"

"Oh, not if you were going to take a break."

Isabella could hear Temmy shuffle around on the other end of the line, probably trying to get more comfortable.

"It's ok. I just didn't feel like working on anything specific. Is there something that you need that I can do?"

Leo shrugged.

"Well, we are trying to find some information for the case we are working on. Issue is the nature of the questions we have, and none of the books in my, admittedly small, collection have what we need."

"What information are you looking for?"

Leo leaned forward in his chair, resting his arms on his knees.

"That's kind of the problem. We need information linked to the practice of Necromancy."

"Oh."

Isabella could tell Temmy wasn't particularly happy about Leo's answer, and could imagine her sitting at their dining room table trying to figure out what to say.

"I can see why you would have trouble finding information. Necromancy is illegal for a reason. There is almost no part of the practice that can be used for anything other than to cause harm or defile the dead."

Leo nodded lacing his fingers together and inspecting the palms of his hands.

"Yeah, I know. I would personally rather not go anywhere near it."

He sighed.

"This is just between the three of us, Temmy, but we believe the person we are trying to find is attempting to create a Reliquary, most likely to hold a fragment of the person creating it."

The other side of the line was completely silent.

"We are trying to find information on the process of crafting a Reliquary and, to some extent, of becoming a Lich. Without that information, it is going to be almost impossible to get a step ahead of this person and find them."

"I see. I could try The Academy Library, but I would have to get permission from the Headmaster to look at anything relevant." Temmy was clearly upset by the idea.

Leo nodded.

"I can message the Headmaster and let him know why we need to look at the information. If you are ok with helping us out, that is. I don't want you to feel like you have to."

"No, it's ok, there is a legitimate need for it. I will try to find something for you."

Leo laid back in his chair, relieved.

"Temmy, you are a saint. I really appreciate it. I will find a nice souvenir for you as thanks and have Isabella bring it to you when she goes back."

"You don't need to do that."

"Of course we do." Isabella said, sitting up again. "And when I get home with that souvenir I am giving you a big hug and making you whole batch of cookies."

"That's too much, Isabella. I really don't need anything."

"Nonsense." Leo declared dramatically. "In fact, you deserve more. I shall get you many souvenirs. And I shall wrap them in the fanciest wrapping paper I can find."

Isabella nodded her agreement.

"And I will make cookies for you every day for a week."

"Please don't. You really don't need to get me anything. I am happy just to help you."

Leo blew a raspberry, placing one hand on his chest.

"And we are just as happy showering you with gifts. Please do not reject that which brings us such great joy."

Isabella picked up Leo's phone and sat up straight.

"As dramatic as Leo is being, he is right. We love you Temmy, let us spoil you once in a while."

"You two. I really..." Temmy paused, too flustered to finish her sentence.

Isabella smiled.

"I will make sure whatever Leo gets you is modest, and he will stick to one souvenir. But I am still going to hug you when I get home, and I am still going to make cookies. You only have to eat one though."

"Alright." Temmy said sheepishly, knowing she wouldn't be able to convince them not to.

Isabella held the phone out to Leo.

"Perfect. Now we just need Leo to catch all the bad guys."

Leo accepted the phone back.

"Can it wait until tomorrow? I'm tired today."

A small, but unmistakable laugh sounded through the phone. Isabella and Leo both grinned.

"You guys are too much."

"We try." Leo said. "Don't worry about having to look for that information until tomorrow. I will message the Headmaster in the morning."

"Ok, I'll speak to him about it tomorrow then."

Isabella laid back down.

"Thank you Temmy. I do hope we get everything sorted out soon. I miss you."

"I miss you too, Isabella. I am sure the two of you will figure everything out."

"We have the blessing of the Great Temmy." Leo declared. "We will solve this mystery quickly now."

Isabella laughed.

"Good, now let Temmy enjoy the rest of her evening in peace."

"Oh, of course. Sorry for taking up so much of your time, Great Temmy."

"It's ok. I don't mind."

Isabella picked up one of the books from her pile.

"Goodnight Temmy."

"Goodnight Isabella. Goodnight Leo."

"Night Temmy."

Leo ended the call and sat his phone back on the side table. He slowly rocked back and forth, staring at the ceiling.

A knock at the door caused him to pause with a confused look on his face for a moment before his face lit up.

"Pizza!"

I I

Chapter Eleven

Leo sat at the dining table, surrounded by books and papers, writing notes in his notebook. He wrote some information down from one of the books and then placed one of the papers in the book to save his place, closing it and setting it aside.

He pulled another book over and opened it, checking one of the papers before leafing through the pages until he found the page he was looking for. He read for a few minutes and then placed the book down next to him and started taking more notes.

Isabella came out of the hallway, drying her hair with a large gray towel. She walked into the kitchen and watched over Leo's shoulder.

"There is a lot going on there." She said, patting her hair between the two ends of the towel.

Leo nodded, finishing another few sentences before setting his pen down and leaning back in his chair with a groan.

"Yeah. Temmy found some stuff to go off of, but it was a really old book that just described the processes and how the magic should flow through everything as you perform it. It didn't, at all, take into account the interactions with using other types of magic. And all Outer Magics are particularly unfriendly towards other types of magic."

Isabella hung the towel over her shoulder and leaned over to get a better look, placing her hand on the table. Her eyes scanned over Leo's notes.

"So you think whoever this is planned out the rituals we saw to facilitate making the Reliquary?"

Leo sighed, leaning forward in his chair.

"It's hard to say. A Reliquary is generally crafted using mercury silver and crystallized Aether. The book Temmy read described how to gather Aether from the environment, but wasn't super clear on how to force it to crystallize. I've been trying to reference how the magic being used to draw in the Aether would interact with other magic. It is starting to look like some parts of the rituals that we were finding weird were probably designed that way to play around those interactions."

Leo flipped back a few pages in his notes and pointed at one section.

"Then again, there are still parts that don't make a huge amount of sense. The deer skulls and other decorations still don't seem to play much of a part here."

Isabella read over the page with a nod, walking around the table to pick up a book.

"Yeah, they are still kind of weird."

Isabella opened the book and skimmed through a few pages, then she paused

"What if it wasn't supposed to be part of the ritual specifically?"

Leo glanced up from his notes.

"Go on."

Isabella put down her book and picked up another one on Native American cultures.

"Didn't Master Dawnheart say something about the tree branches at the first site?"

Leo nodded and flipped further back in his notes.

"Peach symbolizes longevity or immortality. Plum represents pleasantness or young beauty. Cherry could mean good work."

Isabella nodded and turned her book around and placed it on the table in front of Leo.

"Deer are often seen as messengers and providers of life. Immortality, young beauty, good work, and a provider of life. Maybe the person responsible was trying to create an environment that would embody what they were trying to achieve, while also trying to make it look like it belonged with the rest of the ritual site. Maybe to try and lessen the interactions that other magics might cause."

Leo quickly flipped back to a blank page and started writing more notes.

"And what about the second site? What secondary purpose would the second site have?" Leo asked, continuing to scribble notes.

Isabella took one end of her towel and rubbed the side of her head thoughtfully.

"If we think of the deer as a messenger in that case, perhaps they were really just trying to make contact with a spirit?"

Leo shook his head slowly, sitting back and skimming over his notes.

"No, I don't think so. I think it might be something much worse than that."

Leo picked up one of the papers.

"Remember the paper tag we found there? It was one specifically crafted for the trapping of spirits. I think the goal, without telling the guy doing the ritual, might have been to summon Baron Samedi and trap him there."

Isabella frowned.

"That sounds like a really bad idea."

Leo nodded, leaning forward and putting the paper in his hand down. He picked up his pen and started scribbling down another few notes.

"Beyond a bad idea. A patron spirit like The Baron is his own source of Outer Magic, and is far and beyond more powerful than just some random environmental spirit. Not to mention he is an important figure who would likely be summoned by someone else relatively soon. Which would mean having a strong enough seal to hold him, and one strong enough to fight off the magic of other people at the same time. But Baron Samedi is one of the spirits in charge of the dead. There is a belief that if Baron Samedi refuses to dig your grave, that you won't be able to die. For someone who seems to be making an attempt at immortality, that belief might be enough for them to try and force it to happen."

Isabella slowly put her towel down again.

"Do you think they succeeded?"

Leo shook his head.

"No. The Veve they used had too many flaws. They would have been lucky to summon a random spirit, let alone the one they wanted. And I don't think there is a Tao Sorcerer alive who could capture a powerful spirit like that with a single paper tag. If you were stupid enough to try to catch someone like The Baron, it would probably take dozens of tags set up in very specific orientations. Honestly, with a spirit like Baron Samedi, I'm not even certain the laws that govern the spirit world would even allow the magic seals to work in the first place."

Isabella sat down at the table.

"Well that's good I guess. Though I don't really like the idea of someone who would even be willing to try something like that."

Leo nodded, setting his pen down on the table.

"Yeah. People will do really stupid things without considering the consequences if they think it will mean living forever or not getting old."

Isabella sighed, going back once again to drying her hair.

"Well that's just life. Whether we like it or not."

Leo felt his phone vibrate and he took it out of his pocket. He frowned as he saw who was calling him and he put the phone to his ear.

"This is Leo."

Leo listened for several seconds, his expression becoming more and more grim with each word spoken.

"No one saw what happened? And you are certain no magic was involved."

Leo's hand clenched into a fist and Isabella could feel his power rising.

"Right. Thanks for letting me know Titus. We will do what we can on our end to try and track them down."

Leo ended the call and aggressively dropped the phone. He rested his elbows on the table and clasped his hands together, pressing them against his mouth.

Isabella dropped her towel and stood. She quickly moved behind Leo and leaned over, putting her arms around him to support him until he was able to tell her what happened.

Leo spent several minutes in silence, occasionally shaking his head. His power spiked intermittently, but eventually he took a long slow breath and spoke.

"The man who did the rituals, Stanton, was found dead in his hospital bed. He was stabbed. The knife was left in his chest."

Isabella reflexively tensed, but did her best not to squeeze Leo too tightly.

"The nurse checked on him and he was fine. When she went on her rounds twenty minutes later he was gone. The monitoring equipment had been tampered with so it wouldn't set off an alarm when his heart stopped."

Isabella's heart ached, but she stayed quiet and let Leo get the words out.

"Doctor checked him and nothing else was done to him, just stabbed. Probably so that no one would feel magic being used and go to check on him. The only people there were nurses and patients receiving treatment, so they don't really have any leads either."

Leo let his head hang low, and shook it back and forth.

"Izzy, I…"

"Hush."

Isabella interrupted him, knowing where his head would go if she let him continue.

"No apologies. No blame. No regret. We can worry about everything else later. Just take your time, and let yourself be upset."

Isabella waited until she felt Leo nod, then she shifted so she could hug him better and rested her head against his.

They sat silently, unmoving, both doing their best not to think about anything. Minutes passed without them noticing, and eventually Isabella felt Leo put his hand on her arm.

"You smell nice."

Isabella felt her cheeks flush.

"I just showered, so I hope so."

Leo reached up with his other hand and touched the ends of her hair.

"Could I brush your hair for you?"

Isabella slowly stood up straight, letting go of Leo as he half turned in his chair to look at her. His face was almost completely blank and she couldn't tell what he was thinking.

"If you want to. I'll go get my brush."

Leo nodded quietly, and Isabella went to the bedroom and grabbed her brush from her bag. When she came back out, Leo was sitting quietly on the couch.

Isabella gave Leo the brush, then sat cross-legged on the couch with her back to him. He gently pulled all her hair to her back then started brushing from the ends and slowly working his way up.

He continued brushing, careful to work out any knots he found without pulling her hair. Once he reached her neck he finally spoke.

"Thanks Izzy. For letting me do this. I needed something for my hands to do."

"I should be thanking you for doing it for me. I hate brushing my hair after washing it."

Leo nodded, carefully brushing around her ears.

"Yeah? I never really thought about it. You always seem so well put together that I guess it never occurred to me the trouble you have to go through."

Isabella felt one corner of her mouth trying to pull into a smile.

"Thanks. Though at home Temmy does my hair for me most of the time. I haven't really done anything with it for a few days."

"I think your hair is pretty when it's down."

Isabella felt her cheeks flush again, but was starting to realize that Leo was purposely dancing around something.

Leo finished brushing Isabella's hair and held the brush out to her. She accepted it and then scooted around to face him, setting the brush in her lap. They spent several moments in silence, looking at each other.

"Are you alright?" Isabella asked, still having a hard time reading Leo's face, but feeling like he was struggling.

Leo watched her for a moment, though his gaze seemed focused far away.

He slowly shook his head.

"I don't think so."

Isabella pulled the brush off her lap and dropped it on the floor. She slid across the couch and sat on Leo's lap, putting her arms around him and resting her head on his shoulder.

"What do you need?"

Isabella felt Leo put his arms around her and squeeze her tightly, though his arms were shaking.

"I... don't know."

Isabella felt a pang. Leo was always the one who knew what to do or could come up with a plan. For him to feel lost enough not to know made her heart hurt.

"Let's just sit here for a while then. Rushing into things won't help. Let's take our time to think it through."

"Ok." Leo's voice broke, and Isabella held him as hard as she could.

They sat in silence, time slipping steadily by. Minutes turning into hours. Isabella began to wonder if she might be able to coax Leo to fall asleep and get some rest.

She began to gently rock back and forth, humming quietly, slowing her inner power to resonate with his. Leo didn't say anything, just let her rock him. Within minutes, his head lolled forward and Isabella felt his arms start to loosen around her.

She carefully reached out with her mind and slowly filled him with warmth to take away his pain. Leo's arms slowly slid down and he eventually slumped forward.

Isabella sighed quietly in relief, continuing to rock back and forth, content with the idea of supporting him for the rest of the night.

* * *

Isabella's eyes fluttered open and she found herself staring up at Leo's bedroom ceiling. It took her several minutes before she remembered what had happened the night before. She sat up, wondering how she got into the bed, or even how she had gotten into the bedroom.

She carefully removed the covers and slid out of bed, heading over to the bedroom door and peeking out.

The apartment was pretty quiet, but she could hear some papers rustling in the kitchen. She quietly made her way down the hall and found Leo sitting at the table with several hand drawn pages laid out.

"What are you working on?" Isabella asked softly, not wanting to disturb him too much.

Leo glanced over his shoulder at her and then turned back to his papers.

"Good morning, Izzy. I finished compiling my notes and was just laying them out to look at everything."

Isabella walked up behind Leo and placed her hands on his shoulders, leaning forward against the back of his head.

"There is a lot of interactions here."

Leo nodded, making sure to bump into Isabella a few times.

"Yeah. I started to realize that whoever is trying to make this Reliquary must have been planning this out for a very long time. There is so much to account for that there is simply no way to do it without a pretty complex plan."

Isabella put her hands on top of Leo's head and rested her chin on them.

"Can you figure out enough to be able guess at what they are going to do next?"

Leo rolled his head a bit to move Isabella around.

"From what I could piece together, and comparing to what they did to the ritual sites, I think they are getting close to completing it."

Isabella stood up straight.

"Already?"

Leo nodded, standing up with grunt.

"Yeah. They must have done a bunch of other things before these two rituals. Based on how they did these two, this person probably gave rigged rituals to several other individuals to perform. I called Titus earlier and asked him to start looking into past cases that shared similarities to these ones. Strange pieces of the ritual, paper tags, that sort of thing. It may take him a while, but hopefully we will find something that way."

Leo turned around and smiled at Isabella.

"But now I am hungry, so I think I will make breakfast."

Isabella smiled back.

"Breakfast sounds great. I'm glad to see you are feeling a little better this morning."

Leo paused for a moment and then stepped forward and hugged Isabella, pinning her arms to her sides.

"Thanks to you, Izzy. Sorry I worried you."

Isabella stood still, feeling awkward because Leo was preventing her from hugging him back.

"That's fine. I know how you felt. The idea of trying to prevent a death and then having it happen anyway is awful. But that wasn't your fault. It was whoever is causing all of this to begin with."

Leo sighed.

"I know. But I still feel like I could have done more."

"You always feel like that. You have a problem with feeling responsible for things outside of your control." Isabella started wriggling a little. "So let's just do what we can to find the person who is responsible."

"I would be lost without you Izzy."

Isabella scoffed.

"I know that. So are you going to let me hug you back now so we can have breakfast?"

Leo shook his head and tightened his grip.

"Nope. No can do. Not allowed."

Isabella turned her hand around and pinched Leo's leg.

"Ow." Leo complained, jumping back.

Isabella glided past him with her nose in the air and opened the refrigerator.

"That's what you get."

Leo pouted and turned back to the table, gathering his papers and stacking up all the books to move them out of the way.

"Fair enough I guess."

Isabella laughed at him and pulled out a carton of eggs. She cracked some into a bowl and started mixing them with a fork.

"Did I go to bed before you woke up?" Isabella asked, starting to heat a frying pan and adding some salt and pepper to the eggs.

Leo shook his head, carrying a stack of books over to the side table by his rocking chair.

"Nope. You fell asleep on the couch, so I carried you to the bed. I figured you would probably be more comfortable in there."

Isabella paused, remembering Leo falling asleep and realizing she probably did the same thing. She felt her cheeks burning at the idea of Leo carrying her to bed like that.

"Oh, I guess I must have been tired then."

She opened a cupboard to look for something else to put in the eggs and hid her face behind her arm.

"Seems like it." Leo said, sitting back down at the table.

They ate their breakfast and, after Isabella chased Leo away from the dishes, Leo sat down in his rocking chair and started leafing through his notes again.

"So what are we going to do while we wait for Titus to get back to us with the other possible cases?" Isabella asked as she finished drying the last of the dishes and started draining the sink.

Leo sat his notes aside and leaned back, staring at the ceiling.

"Well, I was thinking about it..." He trailed off and just slowly rocked.

Isabella dried her hands and then walked over to Leo, leaning over to look down into his eyes.

"I'm glad to hear you were thinking. Perhaps you could continue to do so."

Leo blinked a few times.

"Oh, sorry Izzy. Feeling a little spacey still I guess."

Isabella walked around and sat on the couch.

"You are forgiven. So what were you thinking?"

Leo slowly rocked, scratching the back of his head.

"I was thinking of maybe performing an Augury."

Isabella leaned back against the couch and crossed her arms over her chest. She considered the statement for several seconds.

"Trying to use some form of far-sight to search could have some results. What would we even look for though? Searching out someone without specific knowledge of that person would be impossible."

Leo nodded.

"This is true. But I came into direct contact with the anchor of a powerful curse. We can look for the source of that curse."

Isabella nodded slowly.

"Yes, I suppose we could do that. Though Augury usually deals with future sight, so looking back would be harder."

Leo grinned.

"I'm sure it will be fine. We can ride the line of the past and present, it shouldn't be too hard."

Isabella tipped her head to one side.

"Temmy would probably help, but that being the case it would be bad to ask Titus to help. We would need one more person. Do you know anyone else who could help?"

Leo nodded again.

"I do. He is on vacation at the moment, so I would have to call him back, but he is already going to be mad at me for not calling him sooner anyway."

"Ooh, your normal partner?" Isabella asked, leaning forward. "I wouldn't mind meeting him. You never really told me much about him, but you seemed to get along with him pretty well."

Leo nodded with a grin.

"Yeah. We get along great. He and I work exceptionally well to-gether. You are probably the only one who I can work better with. Though, I wouldn't want to have to choose between him and Temmy either. I think it would be pretty close."

Isabella's eyebrows rose slightly.

"That's pretty crazy, considering how many years you have been around Temmy."

Leo chuckled.

"Yeah. He and I have a pretty similar thought process. We mesh really well."

Isabella just tilted her head and stared at the floor.

"Well now I'm really curious."

Leo leaned back in his chair.

"I'm sure he will be excited to hear it."

Chapter Twelve

"I'm sorry Alex. Up until a couple of days ago everything was going pretty well."

Leo put his bowl from breakfast next to the sink.

"Well then why didn't you call me a couple of days ago?" Alex complained.

Leo shook his head.

"Even if I had, nothing would have changed. By the time you got all the way back the guy still would have died."

"Still, I could have been there right now. And then we could be doing the Augury."

Leo chuckled.

"And even if you were here at the moment, it still wouldn't make much difference. Izzy took my car to drive back to the Academy last night. She won't be back with Temmy until tonight. We wouldn't be performing the Augury until tomorrow morning, at the very earliest. Delaying a couple days for you to make a return trip won't really change much."

Leo heard Alex scoff on the other end of the line.

"If I leave now I can be back in, like, thirteen hours. We could still do the Augury in the morning."

Leo shook his head again, grinning.

"And Izzy wouldn't let you participate until you got some sleep. I would probably agree with her too."

"Oh, come on. It's not like I haven't worked on no sleep before."

Leo nodded, checking his pockets to make sure he had everything he needed.

"Yeah, same, but Izzy doesn't care. She would make sure we are both rested before using that level of magic. She is a lot more sensible than we are."

"I mean, I guess that is probably true. Well, what is your plan until then?"

Leo grabbed his coat and started putting it on.

"I was just going to spend the day at the office. I haven't really done any paperwork for the investigation yet, at all. Figured I would get that caught up so I wouldn't have to worry about it while we investigate whatever we might see during the Augury."

"Why am I not surprised?"

Leo blew a raspberry as he stepped out his front door.

"You're one to talk. Mister 'waits until Kardinal is breathing down his neck to do his paperwork'."

"Oi, I got all my paperwork done before I left."

Leo nodded, heading down the stairs of the building.

"Yeah, you did. Though I seem to remember you asking me to let you borrow several of my reports."

"Hey, I needed them for research purposes."

"Right."

Leo heard a bunch of movement on the other end of the line.

"Anyway, how are you getting to the office? You said Isabella took your car, right?"

Leo nodded again, stepping out of the apartment building into the parking lot.

"I only live five blocks from Detective Kardinal's office."

Leo heard a clatter and Alex gasped loudly.

"Are you planning on... Exercising!?"

Leo laughed.

"You act like I never do anything. I may be out of shape, but walking a few blocks won't kill me."

"I better hurry back then. I will pray that your heart doesn't stop on the way there."

"Shut up. Even if that happened, Izzy will be back later today. I'm sure she would jump at the idea of breaking a few ribs doing some chest compressions."

"You need to buy that girl some flowers or something. Try to make up for all the crap you put her through so she won't want to break your bones."

Leo shrugged and nodded.

"Yeah, I probably should. I would rather not die sooner than I have to."

"Maybe start with some exercise so you don't have a heart attack."

"I'll exercise more if you cut back on sandwiches."

Silence over the phone was Leo's answer for several seconds.

"Don't even joke about something so sad."

Leo laughed.

"I'll talk to you when you get back. Tell your wife I said hello."

"Leo says hello!" Alex shouted on the other end of the line. "She says hello back."

Leo smiled and shook his head.

"Good bye, Alex."

Alex said good bye and ended the call.

Leo put his phone in his pocket and headed down the sidewalk. He stopped once, about halfway to the office, to sit on a bench and catch his breath.

Eventually he made it to Detective Kardinal's office and went inside, immediately nearly getting run over by a junior detective.

"Sorry Leo," The detective waved and then rushed out the door.

Leo saw Detective Kardinal listening to another junior detective, who was showing him a stack of papers. Leo made his way over and waited until the other detective left.

"Something going on? Need any help?"

Detective Kardinal waved him off.

"No, one of the cases we are investigating just turned into a domestic violence case. Besides, you have your own case to worry about, and plenty of paperwork to do."

Leo chuckled, scratching the back of his head.

"Yeah, I was kind of hoping you would forget that part and let me out of it."

Detective Kardinal shook his head.

"Got to have files on the case, no way around it."

Leo nodded with a sigh.

"Yeah, I know. I figured that's what I would be doing today anyway. But it was a nice idea."

Detective Kardinal nodded, then placed a hand on Leo's shoulder.

"How are you holding up? Do you need anything from me? Having someone lose their life during an investigation is never an easy thing, regardless of who they were."

Leo half smiled, though there was no real emotion behind the smile.

"Thanks. It was a bit rough initially. I admit it would have put me in a real bad place, but I had Isabella with me. She got me through the worst of it."

Detective Kardinal patted Leo on the shoulder a couple times.

"Good. Isabella seemed like a good kid to me when you brought her in. Glad to hear you let her support you. You have a tendency to try and drown yourself in worries."

Leo laughed.

"She told me off for that too. Guess I can't really ignore it if everyone thinks so."

Detective Kardinal smiled at him and turned to go back to his office.

"Let me know if you need anything. Get your paperwork done in the mean time."

Leo half saluted and headed to his own desk. He pulled his notebook out of his pocket and set about the task of transcribing everything over onto official forms.

Some time after noon, the mail was delivered and another detective stopped by Leo's desk and handed him a letter.

"This one's got your name on it Leo."

Leo accepted it with a nod and looked it over. Immediately he noticed the lack of a return address and he felt a knot grow in the pit of his stomach.

He carefully opened the envelope and pulled out the note. Several seconds passed and Leo felt an angry fire growing in his chest. He slowly pulled out his phone and dialed Isabella's phone number, putting the phone to his ear. He heard the operator say that the number was unavailable.

Leo carefully dialed Temmy's phone number and put the phone to his ear. Again, the operator told him the number was unavailable.

An angry red aura settled around Leo as he slowly dialed a third number.

"Leo?" Detective Kardinal carefully approached Leo's desk, and Leo could see the other detectives were all staring at him with worried looks.

Leo held the note out to Detective Kardinal as the person on the other side of the phone answered.

"Headmaster, are Temmy and Isabella still there?"

Several seconds passed and Leo's aura slowly grew into a wildly burning flame. His hands clenched into fists and his eyes squeezed shut.

"They're gone... They took Isabella and Temmy."

* * *

Leo sat quietly, a lamp over his desk the only light in the office. Papers were scattered across the desk, along with two maps. One of Provo city, and the other of the State of Utah.

Leo put his elbows up on the desk and laced his fingers together, resting his chin on his hands. He looked over the papers for the hundredth time, his eyes moving back and forth between the words and the maps, trying to make the wheels in his head turn.

He sighed, putting a finger on the state map and tracing the route between Provo and the Academy. He mentally marked every isolated place along the road, desperately hoping to find where Isabella and Temmy disappeared and where they could have gone.

Leo heard a click as the front door of the office was unlocked and someone carefully entered the room.

"What's wrong Leo? I could feel your power radiating all the way across town."

Leo paused, his finger still on the map.

"Have I really been sitting here so long that you had time to get back, Alex?"

Alex walked over to Leo's desk.

"I sped, and used magic to keep anyone from seeing me do it. What's going on here?"

Leo shook his head, not trusting himself to speak, and pushed a note over to Alex.

Alex picked it up and opened it.

"You will never see your two friends again. I warned you not to keep investigating." Alex scowled. "So that's it. Did Kardinal see this?"

Leo nodded.

"He was here when the note arrived. Police already came here to take statements, and they sent highway patrol to check the road to The Academy, but they haven't been able to find them yet. I... think I scared the other detectives though."

Alex scoffed.

"Sounds right. You feel like the grim reaper, and I imagine it was much worse before you had hours to cool off."

Leo took a deep, ragged breath.

"The police asked me to try and keep control of myself. They already had phone calls coming in from sensitive people across the city when they got here."

Alex nodded, putting the note down.

"I really wish this was a situation where I could laugh about that."

Leo smirked bitterly.

"Would be pretty funny, wouldn't it."

Alex slapped Leo on the back of the shoulder a couple times.

"Well, walk me through what you've got here. Let's figure out where they are so we can laugh about this tomorrow."

Leo shook his head, and waved his hand over the desk.

"I don't know, Alex, I just don't know. I don't have enough information to go off of. The guy we caught was the only one who left any evidence behind. Whoever did this seems to have taken great pains to keep me from knowing what to look for."

Alex gathered up several papers and started reading over them.

"Both rituals had salt circles, did they have markings that could tie them to another system? Or a cardinal direction?"

Leo shook his head again.

"First one was a simple circle with no other adornment. Second was a failed Veve, though a tie in could easily have been hidden there and we wouldn't be able to tell."

Alex shuffled a paper to the back of the pile and kept reading.

"Both rituals done by the same guy?"

Leo nodded.

"He tried to run, but we caught him. He admitted to both rituals, but when I questioned him he claimed he got the instructions for doing the rituals from someone else."

"Did you ask about the person he got the instructions from?"

Leo nodded again, feeling his chest heating up.

"Yeah. He tried telling us what they were doing, but a curse triggered and he ended up in the hospital. By the next day he had been stabbed to death."

"Relax." Alex said, shuffling the papers again to continue reading.

Leo realized his hands were clenched, and his heart was racing. He took a deep breath, opening and closing his hands a few times, and forcing his heart rate and power to slow.

"Sorry Alex."

"No worries."

Alex put down his stack of papers and gathered the rest off of the desk.

Leo's phone went off and he reluctantly answered it.

"Hey Titus."

Leo listened carefully for several moments, grabbing his notepad and pulling his pen out of his pocket.

"Yeah, I can write them down."

Leo wrote down a dozen different city names, adding a number next to each.

"And there were paper tags found in similar places on each of them?"

Leo nodded.

"Ok, thanks for getting back to me."

Leo paused for several moments.

"Yeah, we still haven't been able to find them."

Leo's eyes squeezed closed.

"Thanks Titus, I appreciate it. I'll let you know if I need anything."

Leo ended the call and sat his phone down, rubbing his face with both hands. Alex tapped a line on the page he was looking at.

"This guy said something about a seed. Do you know what that was?"

Leo shook his head, his hands resting over his eyes.

"No. What information we could find never mentioned any sort of seed, so I don't know what they were looking for."

Alex skimmed over the last few lines.

"A place to start the process then? To plant the spell? Or an environ-ment suitable for casting perhaps."

Leo's hands slid away from his face.

"What?"

Alex shrugged, putting the papers down and leaning over the maps.

"Well to seed something is to put it in a place where it can grow. Or you can grow things like crystals by using a little rock or something as a 'seed' for the crystals to attach to. I just figured if they weren't looking for a literal physical seed, maybe what they were looking for was something like that."

Leo sat upright, his eyes darting back and forth as his mind raced through his internal library of knowledge.

Alex glanced over at Leo.

"That's a lightbulb."

Leo shook himself.

"The person we are trying to find is attempting to make a Reliquary. Among the things they need for it is Aether. Something their rituals have been trying to condense out of the air."

Alex nodded.

"Saw the note. What about it?"

Leo carefully rubbed his lower lip, dots beginning to connect in his head.

"Aether is notoriously difficult to work with. For a Reliquary it has to be hardened or crystalized, though I don't really know how to achieve that. But there are other things that can be done with Aether. Something that is even referred to as a seed."

Alex tilted his head to one side.

"You're going to have to explain this one to me."

Leo's eyes continued to drift back and forth, dredging up memories of alchemy classes he had been in years before.

"You can create something called an Astral Seed. A sort of pocket of space, pinched off from the rest of the world."

Alex started to pick up on what Leo was thinking.

"A Reliquary is a complicated thing, and if used for the storage of blood or a soul fragment, it would need to be put somewhere safe where no one would be able to mess with it."

Leo nodded.

"And an Astral Seed, separate from the rest of the world, would be the ideal place."

Alex nodded back, leaning against the desk.

"That would make perfect sense, and fit the definition of a seed. But how feasible is it for them to make one?"

Leo stood up, grabbing his pen and moving his notebook over onto the map.

"Using only Aether? Highly unlikely. But, there is something they can do to sort of cheat in the making of an Astral Seed."

Leo started circling places on the state map from the list he had written down.

"Instead of working with pure Aether, you can use pure natural energy to build on. Essentially increasing the potency of the Aether you are using."

Alex watched Leo work.

"But converting energy into something tangible like that, even for something as thin as Aether, would take a ridiculous density of energy."

Leo nodded.

"Indeed. Exactly like the density of power in a large Leyline."

Alex jumped up, realizing what Leo was talking about.

"So they could take the power directly from a Leyline to create a scaffolding to build on with the Aether."

Leo pointed at Alex with his pen.

"Almost. They could draw it out into a scaffolding directly, but only if they wanted to end up like me, or worse. If they mixed their own power with that of the Leyline they would dilute it too much to use."

Alex leaned over again and planted his hands on the desk.

"So if they can't take the energy out directly they..."

Leo started connecting circled locations with lines, forming a large crescent shape across eastern Utah.

"They manipulate a Leyline, or multiple Leylines, into a position and shape that suits them, then build off of that."

Alex nodded.

"How long would that take?"

"For someone like me who has trained to manipulate stuff like that? Two or three weeks maybe. But someone who doesn't know how to do that would have to do it the hard way. Would probably take them years."

Leo stood up straight and stretched his back. Alex looked over what Leo had drawn. He pointed at the map.

"What are all these circles?"

Leo motioned with his pen.

"These are all the cities that have had rituals performed that were similar to the two here in Provo. Every one of them built in a way that didn't seem to, one hundred percent, make sense. And every one of them had a Taoist paper tag attached to the back of whatever altar or centerpiece was used. If someone wants to move a leyline the only reliable way to move it, outside of manually manipulating it using magic, is faith."

Alex tilted his head to one side.

"Faith? I mean that makes sense here in town, a lot of people and religious groups. But there are places here that are little towns in the middle of nowhere. There would need to be a lot of people involved. Are there that many people in these places?"

Leo nodded.

"Yes and no, but this was designed as a stand in for true faith. These rituals were designed in a way that doesn't seem to make a huge amount of sense, to draw the attention of people. As people focus on the strangeness of the ritual, and exactly where it was performed, a mental pressure is created that creates a force that pulls on the Leylines. The more people hear about each ritual, the more pressure is created. The first ritual Titus found records of, that matched ours, was almost three years ago."

Alex stood up straight again.

"And they picked each ritual site deliberately to push the Leylines in the direction they wanted. That's brilliant. Now how do we figure out where they ended up?"

Leo started tracing lines from each of the circles, following the order he had written down, until all of them converged over a single point.

"They are in the mountains east of Soldier Summit."

Leo picked up his phone and started dialing while Alex rubbed his hands together.

"Always wanted to siege a fortress in the mountains."

Leo put his phone to his ear.

"Well, you are going to get your chance."

Leo pulled his coat off the coat rack and started putting it on.

"Hey Tanya, It's Leo. Tell Master Shepherd and Headmaster Orpheus that we know where to find Isabella and Temmy."

13

Chapter Thirteen

Leo stood under the bright moonlight, carefully breathing in the thin mountain air. Alex scanned over the flat peak they were stood on.

"I can definitely feel a ton of power here."

Leo nodded, reaching out with his mind.

"There is a mass of smaller Leylines tangled with part of the Uinta Line, and it reeks of Outer Magic. This is definitely what we were looking for."

Alex took a deep breath breath through his nose, scrunching it after getting a whiff of something he didn't like.

"Alright, so how do we get in?"

Leo grinned.

"Would normally be pretty difficult. But I forged anchors into the Uinta Line ages ago to move it while I was still at The Academy. I can still feel them here. If you will cast the spells with me, we can force open a gap to get into the Astral Seed."

Alex glanced over at Leo.

"You up for casting like that?"

Leo nodded, his face determined.

"No matter how much it burns, I am getting inside."

Alex smirked, cracking his knuckles.

"Then let's crash this party."

Leo held his arms out, concentrating his power in his chest. A dense, burning red aura rose around him, accompanied by a fierce burning sensation throughout his body.

Alex placed his hands in front of his chest, backs of his fingers pressed together and palms turned up. A vibrant, emerald green aura spreading across his entire body.

Both men lifted their heads, their eyes glowing brightly, and began reciting a string of magic invocations. Their auras merged, creating an enormous flame of iridescent red, green, and yellow hues.

Leo reached out and grasped the anchors he could feel within the Uinta Line, forging magical chains with new anchors embedded in the mountain around them. He raised his arms above his head, closing his hands around the invisible, mental chains.

The air around them grew heavy, and the ground they stood on trembled.

Leo pulled downward on the chains, putting pressure across the Leylines. The air before them began to waiver, distorting as if it was extremely hot.

Alex rotated his hands downward until his fingers were pointed away from him. Then he pressed them forward and started pulling them away from each other, as if trying to pry something apart.

A sound, something between rocks cracking and cloth ripping, echoed over the mountains. The air in front of them tore open in a jagged vertical line, revealing a new scene with muted colors.

Leo pulled the chains tight and sealed them in place, and Alex made a wide motion with his arms before placing his hands back together. Their power slowed, their aura's fading away, until they were left quietly standing before the open tear.

Alex motioned for Leo to lead the way, and they crossed the threshold onto a blank expanse of stone and empty sky.

In the distance stood a tall tower of plain gray stone. There were large, ethereal blue crystals, that seemed to have no defined edge, jutting up around the base of the tower.

Leo could see a figure, wearing a tall hat and carrying a cane, standing in a courtyard in front of the tower.

Leo and Alex walked towards the tower, closing the distance in an almost impossibly short amount of time.

The figure turned out to be a tall, slim, dark skinned man in a nice suit. The figure grinned as they approached.

"I never thought we would have visitors here so soon." The figure removed his hat and bowed. "A pleasure to have you."

Leo nodded politely.

"And who might you be?"

The figure returned his hat to his head.

"You may call me Samedi."

Leo looked the figure up and down, inspecting him carefully.

"You are not The Baron."

The figure's grin grew wider.

"They who summoned me believe that I am. Who am I to deny their belief?"

Alex nonchalantly inspected the fingernails on one of his hands.

"I don't think The Baron would take too kindly to someone using his name inappropriately."

The figure continued grinning.

"What The Baron doesn't know, won't hurt him."

Alex glanced towards the figure, his eyes flashing green.

"I don't take too kindly to you using The Baron's name inappropriately."

The figure's grin grew again, stretching his face to inhuman extremes.

"What care I, for the opinions of mere mortals?"

Alex glanced over at Leo, who merely motioned towards the figure.

"He's all yours Alex."

Alex rolled his shoulders, cracked his neck, and danced back and forth a few times to loosen up his muscles.

"You're about to find out why you should respect the opinion of a 'mere mortal' like me."

Alex placed his two fists together, a green flame enveloping them.

The figure raised his cane like a sword.

"You mortal's, always so quick to..." The figure was interrupted by Alex's fist crashing into the side of his head. A flash of green flame knocked the figure across the courtyard.

The figure twisted in the air, landing on his feet and skidding to a stop, no longer grinning. He dropped the cane, and tossed his hat aside.

"You are a fool, mortal. To believe you can fight a spirit with your bare fists."

The figure began to swell, growing to three times his original size in seconds. His eyes darkened until they were entirely black.

"You will die."

Alex danced back and forth.

"Something you should know about me."

Alex took a step forward, disappearing and reappearing at eye level with the spirit. Another punch sent the figure to the ground, cracking the stone beneath them from the impact.

Alex landed on the ground beside the figure, grabbing him on either side of his head, the green flames around his arms spreading across the figure's body.

"I specialize in fighting spirits with my bare fists."

Alex lifted the figure's head higher, then dropped him and planted another blow to his head as he dropped. The figure roared, then his cries cut off abruptly as his body evaporated in a burst of green flame.

Alex brushed his hands together, the green flames around him disappearing.

"Well that takes care of the guard. Shall we move on?"

Leo nodded.

"We shall. Though..."

They paused, and Alex followed Leo's line of sight to the crystals around the base of the tower.

He inspected the crystals carefully for a moment before he realized there was something inside them.

"Is that... a car?"

Leo grumbled.

"I liked that car too."

Leo shook his head and headed for the tower, Alex close behind. They marched into the tower together, finding nothing but an empty room with a staircase that spiraled along the wall up to another level. They climbed the staircase up to the next level and found an empty room identical to the first.

They carefully climbed a level at a time, finding nothing but empty rooms, until they reach the tenth level.

Leo had to restrain himself as he rounded the corner and saw two individuals laying on the floor, side by side, in the center of the room.

He quickly moved over and found Isabella and Temmy laying together, shoulders touching. He stood quietly over them while Alex joined him, kneeling down and placing his hand on the side of Temmy's neck.

"They are cold, but they are still alive." Alex said. "Something is keeping them asleep though. Wish I could tell you more but, even though I'm a Club, I don't really have any skill with healing."

Leo nodded slowly, forcing his angry doubts out of his mind.

"Do me a favor, Alex. Get them out of the tower."

Alex looked up at Leo.

"What about the person who brought them here?"

Leo shook his head.

"They are probably at the top of the tower. I will take care of it."

Alex stood up, looking Leo in the eye.

"Are you sure?"

Leo nodded.

"Yeah. Besides, I know you used more power on that spirit than you will admit."

Alex grumbled, shaking his head for a moment. He reached out and put his hand on Leo's shoulder.

"Try to keep yourself together man."

Leo half smiled.

"Don't worry about me. As long as you keep them safe, I'll be fine."

Alex shrugged, squatting down and scooping Temmy gently into his arms.

"Try not to keep them waiting then."

Leo nodded and watched Alex head back down the stairs. He spared a few moments to look down at Isabella before turning and starting up the stairs.

Leo slowly marched upwards, each step hardening his resolve. He lost count of the levels he passed, but eventually found himself stepping out into a room that was different from the rest.

This room was filled with a pale, eerie light. At the opposite end of the room was a tall stone throne with fragments of the same ethereal crystals as there were outside the tower.

Above the throne was a silvery armillary sphere with a half formed vial at it's center made of the same ethereal crystal. A stream of glittering, pale blue mist spiraled inward towards the vial, very slowly collecting together into a solidified crystal.

"I will admit, I did not believe anyone could find me here."

Leo finally noticed someone sitting in the throne. It was an older woman with blue gray eyes. Her chest length brown hair was streaked with gray and her skin was dry and papery.

"Though I suppose I should not have underestimated your resolve to find the girl."

Leo felt the words needling at him, but his heart was pounding in his ears, pushing away the anger he wanted to feel.

"So you are the one. The one who caused all this trouble."

The woman raised her arms.

"In the flesh. Though you make it sound as if I merely played some sort of prank. I would hope my work would have left a more lasting impression than that."

Leo shook his head.

"People who commit atrocities should not be remembered for them."

The woman sneered.

"Oh, young man. How nice it must be to be so innocent. I have done nothing but seek survival. It is human nature to try and attain immortality and godhood."

Leo noticed the woman was very thin, and her veins were dark and swollen.

"There are ways to take care of diseases like yours. Cures that are not near as terrible as what you have done. Taking other peoples lives to try and sustain your own is cowardice of the highest order."

The woman scowled angrily.

"You would not think so if it was your own body withering away. Or that of your pretty little girlfriend downstairs."

Leo frowned.

"You have apparently been watching me for some time now. Most likely through some form of far-sight, since you have gone to such great lengths to separate yourself from any of your rituals and I have never seen your face before. So I am sure you are already aware I have had my body wither away once before. I would bet that your tampering with the leylines caused the upset at The Academy almost two years ago."

The woman's scowl turned to a look of pure malice.

"I was almost ready before you set me back by screwing with the leylines. If it wasn't for you I could have been free already."

Leo's expression faded until his face was a blank slate.

"You tie yourself to a blood sacrifice, to craft a Reliquary to hide your soul away. You will never be free again."

The woman slammed her hand down on the arm of the throne.

"I will be immortal! There is no greater freedom than freedom from death. I will take you, along with your friends, and by the end you will wish you could have also been freed from it."

The woman jumped slightly as Leo laughed out loud.

"You can't do anything to me. I am beyond your reach, and you know it."

The woman scowled.

"I pulled that car and its passengers into my world through the leylines. I captured your friends and trapped them here. They couldn't stop me, and neither can you."

Leo smiled, his expression one of spite.

"I am not as passive as Temmy, nor as kindhearted as Isabella. But you already knew that, didn't you? That's why your notes threatened Isabella instead of me. Besides, anyone could perform those feats if they were surrounded by the dense magic of so many leylines. Even without knowing specifics, I can already sense that any cards you would draw at The Academy would be far below average. With the power and skill you currently possess, you would never be able to stand against me."

Leo waved his hand, motioning to the sphere above the throne.

"Besides, you have already committed all your power to finishing the Reliquary. You already knew this, and tried to stall me with conversation. However you can already sense that those you were trying to sacrifice have moved beyond your grasp. I can do whatever I please here and there is nothing you can do about it."

A flicker of doubt played across the woman's face, and Leo frowned.

"I should start by letting you experience every ounce of pain and suffering Isabella and I experienced because of you. Then I should rip out every anchor you have forged within yourself that connects you to the Reliquary. One at a time. Watching you writhe with each new pain as your body and mind are torn to pieces."

The doubt on the woman's face turned to fear, her mouth moving wordlessly.

Leo raised his hand and a dense, blood red aura covered him. The room began to shake as tremendous force caused even the air to respond to his power. His left eye slowly began to glow as he was filled with severe, burning pain.

"Fortunately for you, Isabella, the girl you took to sacrifice, believes my heart is good. My desire to live up to her expectations of me far outweighs my desire for revenge against a creature as sad as you."

The woman's face showed a glimmer of hope, which was immediately dashed as Leo lifted his hand higher, aiming for the armillary sphere. A brightly burning heart appeared in his left eye, exuding it's own brilliant aura.

"So instead, I will simply destroy the Reliquary. Whatever happens to you is merely the consequence of your own actions."

"NO!" The woman reached out towards Leo.

Leo clenched his hand into a tight fist, causing his aura to rush across the room with a bright flash of red flame. The armillary sphere collapsed as if under a great weight and the ethereal crystal at the center shattered into a million fragments, which sprayed across the room and immediately evaporated as the light in the room slowly dimmed.

Leo turned around, his aura fading away, walking back down the stairs as the woman's body turned to ash and fell to dust.

Leo slowly left the tower, walking across the courtyard and heading towards the place where they had entered the Astral Seed. He noticed several silvery cracks forming in the blank expanse that was the sky in this place.

Alex was sitting on the ground near a narrow crack in the air, Temmy and Isabella laying side by side next to him. He waved towards the crack as Leo approached.

"It's mostly closed up, I couldn't get them through."

Leo nodded, kneeling down beside Isabella. He carefully sat her up, leaning her head against his shoulder and reaching around her back and under her legs. He lifted her with a grunt and stood.

"It's alright, Alex. Could you carry Temmy please? I can already feel their presence, even in here."

Alex lifted Temmy up and stood, cutting his own questions short as light started to shine from the crack.

The ground began to shake and the crack began to widen, allowing golden light to spill out into the muted landscape.

Leo led the way and he and Alex stepped back out onto the mountaintop.

Master Shepherd and Headmaster Orpheus stood nearby, each with one arm raised, surrounded by a brilliant golden aura.

"Get clear of the rift you two."

Leo and Alex quickly moved behind the two master sorcerers.

"What do you want to do Orpheus?" Master Shepherd asked, his voice reverberating deeply in the air around them and his eyes glowing a bright metallic gold to match the aura in the air.

Headmaster Orpheus reached out with his second hand, the rift sealing shut.

"Untangle the Leylines. Pull the Uinta Line back in line with the Lesser Dragon Line or we will end up with back pressure all the way up the Great Spiral."

Master Shepherd nodded once and moved his arms in a large, sweeping motion.

The golden aura grew stronger and stronger until Leo and Alex were forced to close their eyes and turn their heads to block out the brightness.

What felt like hours passed before the golden light faded and Leo was able to open his eyes again.

"That should be good enough." Headmaster Orpheus stated. "Thank you for your help today."

Master Shepherd half bowed, a moderate smile on his face.

"I am always happy to help, Orpheus."

They turned and looked at Leo and Alex. Master Shepherd made a motion with one hand.

"Could you take a look at them please, Tanya."

Leo turned around in surprise, not having noticed Tanya standing nearby.

The maid bowed and approached them, placing the back of her hand against Isabella's cheek. After a moment she turned and did the same to Temmy.

"It seems that their vitality was being drained away. It appears Lady Isabella placed both of them under a protective sleep to slow the process."

"Can you wake them?" Master Shepherd asked, Headmaster Orpheus watching silently.

Tanya nodded, turning back to Isabella. She placed both her hands on Isabella's head, a pale green aura settling over her. After several seconds Isabella stirred with a groan, her eyes fluttering open.

"Miss Tanya? What are…" Isabella trailed off, feeling woozy.

Tanya lowered her hands.

"You should take a moment to breath and get your bearings Lady Isabella."

Tanya turned and placed her hands on Temmy's head.

Isabella grumbled, blinking a few times and trying to look around. After a moment she noticed Leo, and her cheeks turned red as she realized he was carrying her.

"Leo? What happened?"

Leo just stared at her face for a few moments, unable to speak, and then pulled her closer, squeezing her tightly against his chest. Isabella sat quietly, slowly trying to piece together her memories.

"Is…Is Temmy ok?"

"Thanks to you, she will be alright." Tanya said, lowering her hands.

Isabella felt relieved and then her view was blocked by someone else. She looked up and blinked in surprise.

"Headmaster?"

Headmaster Orpheus put his arms around Leo and Isabella's heads and hugged them.

"I'm glad the two of you are alright."

Isabella managed to get an arm around the Headmaster to return his hug. They stood quietly for a moment and then Master Shepherd carefully cleared his throat.

"Shall we head back down? Are you two feeling up to it?" He looked back and forth between Alex and Leo.

"I'm good." Alex said confidently.

Leo half chuckled.

"I can manage."

The Headmaster let go of Leo and Isabella.

"Do you need any help, Leo? Your left eye is looking pretty blood-shot."

Leo shook his head.

"I will be alright, I felt some of my power escaping from it earlier, but it doesn't hurt. Could you help Alex though? He was lying. He burned up most of his power in there and he is feeling exhausted."

"Oi." Alex complained.

Leo glanced over.

"Sorry Alex. You aren't fooling me."

Alex pouted, and the Headmaster stepping over and held out his arms, smiling.

"Let me take Miss Artemis for you."

Alex sighed and let the Headmaster take Temmy, who whimpered as she was jostled. The Headmaster nodded, then leaned in close to Alex and whispered.

"Maybe follow Leo down just in case, he isn't much better off than you."

Alex looked at Leo through narrowed eyes.

"I knew it."

Master Shepherd led the way, followed by Tanya, Leo, and Alex. Headmaster Orpheus bringing up the rear.

Isabella sat quietly, bouncing gently up and down as Leo carefully made his way down the mountain trail.

After a while, as the early morning sky grew lighter, Isabella felt something hit her arm. She looked down and found a drop of water.

She looked up, but the sky was clear and some stars were even still visible. She looked back down to see if she had imagined it, and watched as another drop landed on her arm. She looked up one more time and realized Leo had tears in his eyes.

Isabella carefully reached up and absently wiped a tear off his cheek, his cheek immediately turning red.

"Sorry." He said, sniffling slightly.

"Are you ok Leo?"

Leo smiled at her, but his chin and lower lip trembled.

"I thought I lost you." Another tear rolled down his cheek, and Isabella carefully wiped it away. "I'm so relieved I want to curl up and cry."

Isabella felt her throat tighten.

"I'm glad you found us. Thank you for coming to save us."

Leo nodded and his steps slowed.

"You good Leo?" Alex asked, placing a hand on his back.

Leo nodded, coming to a stop.

"I'm good, thanks Alex. Could you give me a minute?"

Alex grinned and snapped his fingers.

"You got it."

Alex walked around Leo and went on ahead.

Leo looked over his shoulder and the Headmaster nodded, walking by without a word. He waited a moment for them to get some distance before speaking again.

"I was so tense today. I haven't felt like that since the accident at the Academy." Leo said and Isabella nodded, not certain what else to do.

"Not until now did I truly realize why. Those who draw King and Queen are often meant to walk side by side, so it makes my heart ache to think about how long it has taken for me to figure it out. I wish I had known to tell you then." Leo took a deep, shuddering breath.

"But I will tell you now, so I never risk losing the chance again."

Isabella's hands curled into fists in her lap and she felt her heart pounding in her chest.

Leo looked down and smiled, his eyes filled with tears.

"I love you, Isabella."

Isabella did her best to smile back, her vision blurring as her own tears started to stream down her face.

"I love you too, Leonidas. More than anything."

Leo pulled her close and hugged her tightly.

"I... hope I can make it down the mountain."

Isabella laughed, placing a hand on his face and planting a kiss on his cheek.

"I wouldn't mind so much if you don't."

Epilogue

Leo stood outside the Academy gate, stretching his back and enjoying the warmth of the sun. He nearly got knocked over when Alex walked up behind him and smacked him on the back.

"Tired of the party already?"

Leo chuckled.

"No, just needed a breath of fresh air. And I am waiting for another guest to arrive."

Alex nodded.

"Oh that's right, we are still waiting for..." Leo clamped his hand over Alex's mouth, looking around.

"Shhh. Keep it to yourself. I don't want Temmy to know yet."

Alex drew an X over his heart and raised his hand as if he was taking an oath.

Leo let go and wiped his hand off on his pants.

"I'm glad you and your wife could make it though."

Alex scoffed.

"Of course we were going to show up for your wedding. What do you take me for?"

Leo laughed.

"I appreciate it nonetheless."

Alex shrugged.

"Well, what can I say? Got to keep the people happy."

Leo shook his head with a grin and Alex tapped him on the shoulder, pointing at the entrance.

"Speaking of which."

Leo turned around and found Isabella standing at the entrance door in her pink silk dress. He waved her over and Alex saluted.

"I'll leave you to it then. Good luck."

Leo returned the salute.

"Thanks Alex." Isabella said, Alex tipping a non-existent hat to her as he passed.

She walked over to where Leo was standing and gave him a quick kiss.

"Is he here yet?"

Leo shook his head.

"Not yet. But he left quite a while ago, so he should be here any time. What about Temmy?"

Isabella pushed a stray strand of hair behind her ear.

"I had someone go tell her to meet me out here."

Leo nodded, motioning with his chin towards the entrance.

Temmy was leaving the building, trying to hold her pink skirt up off the ground, and Isabella waved excitedly.

"Temmy! Your hair looks so good in the sun with your dress. Have I told you that you make the cutest bridesmaid ever?"

Leo could see Temmy's cheeks turning a shade similar to her dress.

"Yes. I think you have told me ten times now today."

Leo mock gasped.

"What? Only ten times? Izzy, that's not nearly enough. Are you feeling well?"

"Please Leo, you don't need to encourage her." Temmy said, looking down at the ground.

Leo grinned and then saw a police car driving down the main drive towards the entrance.

"Izzy, he's here." Leo said, his grin quickly fading.

"Who?" Temmy asked, looking up to see the car approaching.

Isabella turned and put her arms around Temmy.

"I just want you to know we love you and are right behind you."

Temmy got a worried look on her face.

"What? What's going on?"

Leo smiled at her and carefully pulled Isabella away.

"Someone I work with wanted to come to our wedding, and I think it is important that you meet him. And I know we are probably making you more nervous by acting like this, but please trust us. We are behind you one hundred percent, so be brave Temmy,"

Temmy frowned, clearly unhappy, but started walking towards the police car as it parked.

The car door opened and an officer in full uniform with coppery black hair stepped out, placing a hat on his head and closing the door behind him.

Temmy's steps faltered and she came to a stop as Titus approached her. His expression was sober as he stopped a few feet away from her.

After a few moments of tension, Titus carefully got down on his knees and bowed his head to the ground.

"I do not deserve forgiveness, especially not from you. Every single thing I did at the Academy was despicable. For that, I am truly sorry."

Several minutes passed in silence and Isabella buried her head in Leo's shoulder to hide. Titus kept his head down on the ground and simply waited.

"You... should come inside. That's where the reception is." Temmy finally spoke, her voice barely audible.

"With your permission." Titus said, finally raising his head.

Temmy paused for a moment and then nodded.

"Fantastic." Leo called out. "Seriously Titus, couldn't you have driven a little faster? Flip the lights and the siren on or something?"

Isabella rushed over and hugged Temmy, letting her hide her face from Titus. Titus carefully stood up and brushed off his knees.

"Police officers have to follow the law too, Leo. I drove the limit the entire way."

Leo grinned and put his arm around Titus's shoulders, steering him towards the entrance.

"Well, at least Charlie will be excited to hear her brother finally arrived."

Titus frowned.

"Wonderful."

www.ingramcontent.com/pod-product-compliance
Lightning Source LLC
Chambersburg PA
CBHW070355200726
48294CB00003B/928